P9-DDD-157

A Treasury of Glorious Goddesses

Call Me Athena

Greek Goddess of Wisdom

by Shirin Yim Bridges

Illustrations by Shirin Yim Bridges

For Juliet, on her first birthday.

Series editor **Shirin Yim Bridges**
Editor **Susan Lyn McCombs**
Copy editor **Jennifer Fry**
Typeset in Adobe Caslon Pro and Volkswagen
Illustrations rendered in pen and marker
Photographs unless otherwise indicated are in the public domain, used courtesy of the Creative Commons, or licensed from Shutterstock.
We sincerely thank all contributors to Wikimedia Commons.
Manufactured in the U.S.A.
Library of Congress PCN: 2014931200
ISBN: 978-1-937463-94-6
First Edition 10 9 8 7 6 5 4 3 2 1
Goosebottom Books LLC
543 Trinidad Lane, Foster City, CA 94404
www.goosebottombooks.com

Cast of Main Characters

Athena	Goddess of Wisdom
Zeus	King of the Gods
Hephaestus	The Smith God
Ares	God of War
Hera	Goddess of Marriage
Poseidon	God of the Seas
Aphrodite	Goddess of Love and Beauty
Demeter	Goddess of the Corn
Apollo	God of Music
Artemis	Goddess of the Hunt
Hermes	The Messenger God
Dionysus	God of Wine
Arachne	Lydian princess
Jason	Greek hero
Diomedes	Greek hero
Odysseus	Greek hero
Achilles	Greek hero

My Father's Headache

The family joke is that I was one big headache from the start. I can tell you the story, but I can't vouch for it. All I remember is standing in a room, the smell of ozone in the air, looking down at gods and goddesses cowering on a marble floor.

The story goes that my father, Zeus, woke up one morning with a gnawing pain behind his left eye. Throughout the day, it got steadily worse. Hurling a few thunderbolts didn't make things better—and that usually works for Dad. He scares a few people, feels like the big man, and goes back to being his blustering self. A spin in the chariot didn't help either. Although Dad whipped his horses across the heavens, making everybody down below run for cover, he only came home exhausted and in an even worse mood.

Dad in a bad mood is not good news for anybody. Down below, the world experiences his displeasure as tempests that strip trees and flatten crops. Hailstones the size of your fist pulverize stone temples. Lightning sets forests and hillsides ablaze. But up here, it's even worse. Before Dad unleashes his rage, we have to sit through the building tension. We have to watch those brows furrow and knit in slow increments and worry about how to unknit them. Everybody speaks more softly, moves more gingerly. Nobody wants to be the last straw that triggers Dad's outburst.

So on that day, when Dad swept into the throne room with a face like a purple thunder-cloud, all of the hangers-on scattered. The *nymphs* slipped back into their rivers and woods, the *nereids* retreated to the bottom of the sea, and the *satyrs* scurried away to find another party.

Of course, the gods and goddesses were not so lucky. Their duty was to remain in attendance, whatever Dad's mood. All they could do was watch as their mighty leader climbed onto his high throne. He hunched there, glowering at them as they tried to blend in with the columns.

Dad's face was clenched like a fist. The pain behind his eye got so bad that he finally screamed at the Smith God, Hephaestus, to cleave his head with an axe. Hephaestus stumbled forward, unsteady from lameness and terror—then hesitated. (I mean, wouldn't you?) Dad let out an enormous roar. In panic, Hephaestus swung his axe. There was a clap of thunder and an even-louder shout. The room exploded with lightning. Everyone threw their arms around their heads and dropped to the floor. And—the walls still ringing from my war cry—I, Athena, Goddess of Wisdom, stepped fully grown and clad in armor from my father's forehead.

At least that's how the story goes.

You Can't Choose Your Family

I was still slightly dazed from my arrival as Hephaestus led me away from the throne room through a maze of marble corridors. He leaned on two golden crutches as he walked. His spindly legs, barely thicker than the apparatus supporting them, had been irreparably broken in a fall when his mother, Hera, threw him out of heaven.

The knowledge of his terrible fall seeped into my mind as we walked, like smoke filling a room. It's called *omniscience*. It's one of the cool things about being a goddess. You can know anything. All you have to do is concentrate. There's one exception—and of course I automatically knew this too. You can't look into your own future. You can't see your own fate, which is just as well because you can't change it. Nobody can.

Hephaestus stopped at a carved wooden door.

"Your rooms," he said, pushing the door open with a flourish.

I stepped into a well of light. Tall windows faced us, letting in sun and air. A medley of cubbyholes, shelves, and drawers lined the other walls. To the right, stood a large desk. To the left, double doors opened into a bedroom. Two comfortable couches beckoned beneath the open windows.

"Thank you," I said. I knew Hephaestus had designed the rooms, and I loved them.

He nodded, pleased.

"Dinner will be served exactly fifteen minutes after you hear the gong," he said. "My mother doesn't like it if you're late." He turned and hobbled away.

Watching him leave, I wondered why Hephaestus didn't shape shift into an athlete with strong legs. That's another advantage of being a god or goddess—you can become anything you want. But shape shifting, like omniscience, takes concentration and energy. Besides, Hephaestus looked happy enough being who he was.

I wandered over to the windows. They looked out onto a lawn that sloped down to the edge of a cliff. Beyond the cliff there was nothing but clouds. Everything felt crystalline and still, as if I were all alone in the world. It was an eerie, almost scary feeling. Then the sound of the gong came reverberating down the halls.

I stepped into the bedroom and slipped off all my armor. There was no time to change my *chiton* now. I'd just have to go in the robe I had on. I picked up a hand mirror of polished brass from my bedside table. Grey eyes. A strong nose that was just shy of being masculine. Dark brown curls—at least I didn't have helmet hair.

Only two minutes later, I'd found the dining room. *This should start me off on Hera's good side,* I thought. It was smaller than the throne room, but had the same marble floors and columns. It would have been a cold room if it were not for four bronze braziers, one in each corner, throwing out firelight and the crack and crackle of burning logs.

I struggled to pull out a chair at the massive wooden table in the center of the room. This was hardly the graceful first entrance I'd hoped to make.

From across the table, my half-brother Ares, God of War, looked up at me.

"Well, well, well, the goddess of wisdom," he said, giving me a lopsided grin. "How wise can you be when you're only a few hours old? Welcome to the 'O's."

The "O"s was Ares' name for our family, the Olympians. He had nicknames for everybody.

I gave him a relieved smile in return. Of all the gods and goddesses, I'd expected Ares to be the least happy to see me. He was already the god of war, and here I sprang, not just the goddess of wisdom but also of wartime strategy. Many would have seen this overlapping of our powers as me stepping on his turf. But not Ares. I soon learned that he doesn't take anything too seriously.

"If you hadn't sprouted forth fully clad in armor, I would have taken Hephaestus' axe to you myself," he joked. "Talk about causing a drama." He rolled his eyes.

"But look at Big Daddy-O over there," he laughed. He pointed to our father, Zeus, at the head of the table—broad chested, big nosed, with a full mop of wavy hair like motion lines around his head, radiating vigor. Every one of Dad's lightning bolts releases several billion joules of energy. He might casually throw eight million bolts to earth in one day, like shaking off crumbs after dinner. That's power. But at that moment, Dad was stealing glances at me like a bashful schoolboy.

I wished he would come over and say hello instead. *Dad*, I pleaded silently, *I don't know anyone here.* His omniscience could have told him what I was thinking, but he wasn't paying attention to that. He was too busy getting his head around the physical reality of me, a goddess he had produced all by himself.

"Look at him! You'd think you were his brainchild!" Ares laughed at his own joke, slapping the table. "Come on, sit down."

I did sit down, but then struggled again to pull in my chair. The twelve chairs around the table had been designed to look like thrones, but they were heavy and uncomfortable. I looked around to see if anybody else was having the same problem. Next to Dad, my uncle Poseidon stared at me with open irritation.

"What's his problem?" I asked Ares.

"Ah, U.P.," said Ares, as if that explained everything.

Uncle Poseidon always looks like a grumpier version of Dad, but you can tell them apart because Dad carries a lightning bolt and Uncle Poseidon (U.P. or "you pee"—which makes Ares hoot with laughter every time) carries a trident. When he throws that trident, U.P. can change the shapes of lives and continents in an instant. The earth shakes, buildings topple, and tsunamis sweep away everything before them.

Right then, U.P. looked like he wanted to throw his trident at *me*. I guess he really didn't like being made to cower on the floor.

Dad's wife Hera, seated on Dad's other side, didn't look too happy to see me either. I tried to give her an *I'm here on time* smile, but she dropped her dark lashes over her famous cow eyes and looked away as if I had a prominent booger.

I now know that Hera, whom Ares nicknamed Mrs. O, must have been seething inside. She's the goddess of marriage but, ironically, she is doomed to an eternity of unhappiness being married to Dad. Big Daddy-O believes that monogamy is not for the gods, and certainly not for him. He's had a string of mistresses and refuses to apologize for any of them—or for the children he's had with them. So, every night, Mrs. O has to sit down to dinner with some of Dad's children who are not her own: the archer twins, Artemis and Apollo, Goddess of the Hunt and God of Music respectively; Hermes, the Messenger God; Dionysus, the God of Wine—and now me, born from her husband's head without any help from her at all.

Luckily, at this point Hephaestus scraped back the chair next to mine with his powerful arms and struggled to fold his legs under the table. He's one of Mrs. O's sons, but she looked at him as if he had a nose booger even bigger than mine. His wife Aphrodite, Goddess of Love and Beauty, coming to the table at the same time, ignored him and settled as lightly as a butterfly on the chair next to Ares.

"So, you're not only the goddess of wisdom, but also of crafts—of weaving and carpentry?" Hephaestus gushed, as if these powers were far more impressive than boring old wisdom.

"I am," I replied. "And with chairs like these, you could use a goddess of carpentry around here."

He chuckled. He pulled a small, exquisitely made silver box from his pocket and put it on the table between us. He ran a finger over its filigreed surface and a little drawer slid open.

"Oh my," I said.

He grinned at my response. He showed me more hidden latches, triggering doors, drawers, and secret compartments that sprang open.

I was mesmerized by the intricate craftsmanship—until Ares guffawed. I looked up to see Aphrodite covering her mouth with a graceful hand as she laughed her tinkling laugh. She had twisted around on her chair to face Ares. Now she leaned forward and touched her forehead to his shoulder, as if embarrassed by something she'd said. I could not believe they were flirting with each other so openly—right in front of Hephaestus—or that the family carried on as if nothing was happening.

What is going on? I thought.

Aphrodite straightened up and smoothed a strand of hair from her face, still laughing.

Her eyes met mine. Her gaze was icy.

I redirected my attention to the half-brother and new friend beside me. Hephaestus gave me a watery smile and sprang open yet another secret compartment. His smile deepened with satisfaction. Finally, after carefully closing all the tiny doors and drawers, he placed his handiwork beside my plate. "Welcome to The Twelve," he said.

The Twelve Olympians: Zeus, Poseidon, Hera, Artemis, Apollo, Hermes, Me, Dionysus, Hephaestus, Aphrodite, Ares, and Aunt Demeter, Goddess of the Corn, who at that moment entered the room.

I love my aunt. She's invariably kind. Her eyes swept over everyone, looking for me. With one glance she saw that I was feeling awkward and motherless—a clumsy cuckoo who didn't belong in the nest. She came straight over and sat down on my other side.

"What has clever Hephaestus made for you?" she asked, encircling both of us in the warmth that she shed like a lamp.

I held the little box out on the flat of my hand. Hephaestus proudly pointed out how to find the secret latches.

"How fabulous!" Aunt Demeter exclaimed. "Apollo, Artemis, have you seen this?"

She leaned down the table and directed Hermes and Dionysus to look also. Soon, she had them all drawn into conversation. Nobody seemed particularly interested in speaking to me, but at least the room felt less frosty.

As Hephaestus had promised, precisely fifteen minutes after the gong, dinner was served.

"Here, this is a good bit," Aunt Demeter said, choosing an extra-nice morsel of charred beef from a serving dish and setting it on the side of my plate.

I turned to thank her, but tears suddenly pricked my eyes. I had to look away.

I don't think anyone can normally accuse me of lacking confidence. You know what it's like starting a new school, right? Well, imagine starting a new life—and being plunked in the middle of it so abruptly. It's a bit much even for a goddess.

Aunt Demeter took my hand under the table and gave it a squeeze.

"Everything will be OK," she said.

It had to be. Whether anybody liked it or not, I had arrived.

A City in My Name

I settled in on Mount Olympus, but slowly. It was hard to not feel like an outsider. The family didn't go out of their way to be mean or to exclude me, but they'd had their routines for thousands of years. They saw no reason to change now.

Hephaestus spent the days down in his workshop on the island of Lemnos. He'd landed there when he was thrown from Olympus, and now it was his second home. Nobody ever spoke about why Hera had thrown him out in the first place, but I found it interesting that Hephaestus seemed to have forgiven her completely, while she obviously still disliked him. I would have thought it'd be the other way around.

Aunt Demeter was also always down below, because that's where the corn was. On any given day, there was a sowing or a reaping that she had to go to supervise.

I looked forward to seeing Hephaestus and Demeter every evening, but I didn't quite know what to do with my days. Dad rescued me from my limbo.

"Come and make yourself useful," he boomed from my doorway one morning. He was acting extra blustery because he still felt a little shy around me.

"You're the goddess of wisdom," he said, marching down the corridor so quickly that his robes swirled behind him like storm clouds. "You can help me decide cases in the throne room."

It was an interesting job. Every morning, I'd take my place beside Dad's throne. I listened quietly as gods and lesser immortals petitioned their supreme leader for justice. Sometimes we also heard prayers from the mortals down below. I began to see how gods and mortals and their worlds intertwined. For the most part, it wasn't a close or loving relationship. They saw us more as a form of insurance. If they kept us happy, we'd keep the worst disasters away. On our side, we saw them mainly as providers of burnt meat and fat, savory supplements to our divine fare of nectar and ambrosia.

Another thing I learned was how to read Dad. I knew to never say a word unless he turned around and cocked an eyebrow at me first. As time went on, Dad started cocking his eyebrow more and more. He'd often grunt with satisfaction after he heard what I had to say. Once, we disagreed on an issue. We didn't raise our voices, but they got steely. The other gods and goddesses glanced away. I lifted my chin and held Dad's gaze. That locking of eyes when everyone else was afraid to even look kindled a special connection between us. He'd had a soft spot for me from the start, but now mixed in with affection and pride was a little secret respect.

My relationship with U.P., on the other hand, grew more and more tense. He found me disrespectful because I believed I was his equal. I was a whole generation younger and a woman, so U.P. thought I was nuts. *Why should age and sex make any difference?* I thought. U.P. took my attitude as deliberate insolence.

One day, U.P. came to the throne room to petition for ownership of a city.

"This *polis*," he said, pointing to its place on a map, "is going to become a great naval power. I'm the ruler of the seas, so it should come under my protection."

"No!" I blurted out. I'd been watching that city with interest, too.

"Excuse me?" said U.P.

Dad cocked an eyebrow.

"I'm sorry, but that isn't just a naval city." I knew I'd started on the wrong foot, but what I was about to say was true—and in my opinion, obvious. "It's not like its rival, Sparta, which is mostly focused on war and power. This city is also blooming with new ideas, expressed in literature, philosophy, theater, and politics.

"One day," I said, using my omniscience, "it's going to become the birthplace of democracy. I'm the goddess of wisdom. The city should belong to me."

"You have to be joking!" U.P. spluttered. His eyebrows bristled like the back of a cat. It wasn't just that I wanted "his" city, but I was challenging him for it in public—in front of the gods and demigods who were now shifting their weight nervously.

"Call your pup to heel," he snapped at Zeus.

Dad steepled his fingers and looked at both of us. He's usually judge and jury in matters like this. Sometimes, he tries to be a fair judge. Sometimes, he openly plays favorites. Today, Dad just looked exasperated.

"It's only a city," he said to U.P. "It's not as if you don't have all the seas and oceans as your domain."

"That's not the point!" U.P.'s thick finger jabbed the air, as if dotting an exclamation mark.

"The point is, this is a naval power. I am lord of the seas. I am the senior and more powerful god. And I claimed it first."

"The people of this city really value thinking," I spoke up.

U.P. howled. His eyes boggled in disbelief that I was even being allowed to speak.

I continued, "They will be unique in how they structure their government, and how their daily lives will revolve around debate and discussion."

Dad grunted. It was a dismissive sound and U.P. turned to him with hope, but actually Dad was dismissing the case entirely.

"As you both want the city, why don't you see which of you the city wants?"

Dad chuckled, warming to his own idea. "Democracy, right? Each man gets his vote? Let's give them a first taste. Let's see whom they'll vote for."

Great, I thought. *Family dinners are going to be even more awkward now.*

An hour later, U.P. and I stood on a flat-topped rock, almost 500 feet above the sea and four miles inland, with a distant view of a sparkling harbor. The city's people were assembled in a wide semi-circle before us. They regarded us with a mixture of awe and dread—and also a little annoyance. After all, they hadn't asked to give their city to a god. They were doing perfectly well without a patron. And now, here they were, corralled together at the last minute by Hermes and told to make a decision that was surely going to displease at least one of the great Olympians.

Dad handed down the rules: U.P. and I each had to give the city a gift. Based solely on our gifts, the people would choose which of us could call the city his or her own. Dad then went off for a chariot ride, having solved the problem as far as he was concerned.

I had to hand it to U.P., he knew a thing or two about making an impression. Without saying a word, he stepped forward and drew himself to his full height. Power flowed from him in waves. Raising his trident with a muscular arm, he smote the earth before him with a resounding crash. As the reverberations faded away, we heard a deepening rumble. Then, the ground cracked open where it had been struck and a plume of white water burst forth, followed by another, and another. Great jets of seawater arched out, morphing into the necks of salt-white horses that galloped forward snorting and tossing their manes, until they were assembled eight abreast. Behind the horses, the spring continued to pulse. Poseidon's message was clear. He could bring the power of the ocean and the finest warhorses. He could make his city invincible by sea and by land.

U.P.'s spectacle was so successful that it took a few minutes for everybody to remember that it was now my turn. With a shuffling of feet, they turned around to face me.

No time like the present, I thought, and prodded the rock beside U.P.'s fountain with the tip of my spear.

There was no reverberating crash, no ominous rumbling. In fact, at first, nothing seemed to happen at all. Then from the ground rose a curled leaf, followed by a tender stem, followed by more leaves and stems in quick succession. Within minutes, in a great unfurling, a tree rose from the ground. It bowed gracefully toward its audience, its leaves twinkling silver.

Silence. Even Poseidon was struck dumb. A tree? What kind of gift was that?

I stepped up to the tree and picked one of its small, perfectly oval fruit. Then I broke off a slender branch heavy with leaves. I walked over to the people. I don't think the gods had ever walked among them before. Even Hermes in his duties barked his news or directions from a distance. I waded into the middle of the crowd and showed them the olive in my cupped hand. Our heads bent together over my offering.

"See this," I said, holding the olive aloft. "This

is food. This can see you through hard times."

A murmur passed through the crowd.

"And this," I added, squeezing the olive until a single bead of golden oil hung from it like amber, catching the sun. "This is oil. It is food, too, but it is also medicine, heat, and light."

I extended the olive branch to them. "This," I said, "will forever be the symbol of peace. Make a gift of this to both your friends and your enemies, and peace will bring you wealth."

Eager fingers reached out to touch the leaves, brushing my hands and arms. I twisted the branch into a wreath.

"With this," I concluded, "you will crown your heroes and your brides."

By now the people were pressed close around me. Their faces were flushed. In their minds, my words took wing. They glimpsed a future full of every-day triumphs: tables groaning with food; families gathered; children laughing; time free from war to cultivate olive groves—and prosperity.

An old man laid his hand on my arm. "You," he said, "are our goddess."

U.P. was fit to be tied. He didn't dare strike out against the city. Zeus himself had laid down the rules, and U.P. lost fair and square. So, simply to spite me, he hurled huge waves across the Thriasian Plain, whose people were loyal to me and completely unprepared for the floods he sent their way. They watched as their fields of grain were engulfed by water. They fled as the earthen walls of their homes melted and tumbled into the new inland sea.

I found the Thriasians homes in my new city. My new people welcomed them. For me, they built a small stone temple on the flat-topped rock where I had planted that first olive tree. Over the years they added more buildings, until it became not one temple but an *acropolis*—an upper city—dedicated to me. They built a grand flight of steps up to it and an entranceway of imposing columns. At one time, a colossal bronze statue of me, three stories tall with spear raised and ready, could be seen glinting in the sunlight as you approached by sea. Behind the statue lay the magnificent Parthenon, still considered the highpoint of Greek art and architecture, built to thank me for guiding the Athenians to victory at the famous Battle of Marathon.

Yes, the *Athenians*. They renamed their city Athens to show their love for me. The feeling was very, very mutual.

The Vote

Back up on Mount Olympus, nothing much was said about my tussle with U.P. over Athens, or his vindictive strike against the people of the plains. I was starting to learn that this family avoided talking about anything unpleasant, which was especially frustrating to me as the goddess of wisdom, because it's hardly *wise*. Hera's treatment of Hephaestus, Dad's treatment of Hera, Aphrodite's flirtation with Ares—all these topics were simply not mentioned. Now, everyone deliberately didn't mention the conflict between U.P. and me. Worse, to avoid stumbling onto the issue, they stopped using words that started with "Ath" altogether—not just *Athens* but also *Athena*.

Instead of staying on Olympus and suffering the cold shoulder, I spent a lot of time down in

Athens. I liked being around the Athenians who were always in the process of changing—always playing with new ideas, or finding new ways to express themselves. They were so unlike my family who had all of time yawning before them. When you know you'll be around forever, there's no great hurry to change anything too quickly. But the Athenians were hungry to change, to learn; and I loved to teach. I taught them the use of the plough, the rake, the ox-yoke, the horse-bridle, and the chariot—all of which I invented. My desk was covered with scrolls of my drawings, plans, and designs. I worked with their carpenters and shipwrights. I taught the women cooking, weaving, and spinning. I introduced the Athenians to the earthenware pot, which in their hands became much more than a practical vessel. It became high art, decorated with black or red figures in silhouette, depicting scenes from both everyday Athenian life and the lives of the "O"s.

I brought some of this beautiful pottery

back up to Olympus as a gift for Aunt Demeter. A few nights later, coming to dinner in the lofty, columned hall, I found the table set with dishes I had given her. Before each seat was a small painted bowl holding a mound of black and green olives slick with oil. Eyes darted at me as I pulled out my chair, and at U.P. who sat squinting at the olives before him.

I glared at Ares, thinking that maybe setting the table with olives was one of his bad jokes. He examined his olives with unfeigned innocence.

At the head of the table, Dad was intent on extracting the largest, juiciest olive from his bowl. He popped the olive into his mouth. He spit the pip out delicately between thumb and forefinger, and placed it on the table. He chewed thoughtfully, then repeated the test with another olive. "They're really quite good," Dad announced, wiping his fingers on the tablecloth.

A murmur of agreement went around the table.

"So," Dad said, turning his attention to me,

"you've won yourself a city with a...what is it? Is it a vegetable or a fruit? A berry?"

"It's a fruit," I replied.

"A fruit. So, you've won yourself a city with a fruit."

"Not just the fruit, Dad, the tree."

"She's right," my aunt Demeter chimed in. "The fruit is great food and especially useful because it can be cured and stored. However, the oil is arguably even more valuable—not just as food, but as cooking and heating oil, and for use in lamps; not to mention its use in soaps, cosmetics, and medicines. And then there's the wood. Athena's tree really is the gift that keeps on giving."

"So you think the tree was the better present?" Dad asked her.

"I do," Aunt Demeter answered firmly, but he had already started nodding. I had the feeling the whole exchange had been rehearsed between them.

"And who else here agrees with Demeter?"

One by one, the goddesses raised their hands.

"Who thinks Poseidon should have won and is justified in his sulk?"

Ares shot his hand up, happily sucking on an olive.

"Oh come on!" he laughed, when nobody else made a move. "It might be useful, but it's just a tree! Who ever heard of a tree beating victory in war?!"

Of course war was more important than a fruit tree when it came down to it. Or at least it felt like it should be more important. The rest of the gods raised their hands.

"Ah well, an even split," Dad blithely miscounted. It was actually four goddesses against five gods, with me, U.P., and Dad not voting. "The mortals voted the way they voted. Our own vote has proven that the contest could have gone either way. So, there's no excuse for any sulking."

He flicked his olive pips off the table and watched them roll to a stop on the marble floor. Without looking up he said, "Stop destroying other people's cities or I'll flatten all of yours."

U.P. grunted.

"As for you, Athena," Dad said, breaking the ban on "Ath" words, his voice deepening into a growl, "watch how close you get to those mortals. Moving among them might seem harmless, but they get confused. Familiarity makes them forget respect. Any disrespect to one of us is an insult to all and will not be tolerated. Am I clear? Don't let a situation develop, because believe me, I'll fix it with a lightning bolt."

"Yes, Dad," I said.

Too Close

Of course I went back to spending my time among the mortals. I had no idea what Dad was worried about. There was no disrespect; the people loved me. His insistence on being feared was so old fashioned. I went on bringing my crafts to towns dotted all across the Ancient Greek World, which was much larger than Greece itself. It included city-states like Ephesus and Troy, and countries like Lydia and Caria, all of which are in modern Turkey.

Nowhere were my skills more appreciated than in Lydia, famous for its purple dye and its markets noisy with the barter of fabrics and luxury goods. In the *gynaikon*, or women's rooms, of the Lydian palace, I met regularly with the ladies of the royal house. In the Greek world at that time, girls and women were forced to stay at home and spend their days in the gynaikon. As a goddess, however, I roamed wherever I pleased. I couldn't imagine being cooped up in the same rooms day after day. But if it was a cage, the gynaikon of the Lydian palace was an exquisitely gilded cage, and it had an informal, friendly prettiness that was a welcome change from the elegant and imposing halls on Olympus.

The room was airy, with high ceilings. The splashing of water fountains drifted in with the breeze from the gardens below, stirring the fine gauze curtains that hung at every window to soften the glare of the sun. Painted patterns decorated the walls in the sparkling colors of a peacock's tail. Couches and *divans* were scattered among the looms that the women used for their weaving. Towers of sweets, cakes, nuts, and fruit, and jugs of cool water and wine waited on small tables. I immediately felt at home.

In this private place, away from men and

prying eyes, the Lydian women literally let down their hair. "Come, you too, Athena," they coaxed on my third visit. I let them brush out my tresses and braid them with flowers and sweet-smelling herbs. I hoped Dad wasn't turning his omniscience my way.

As the weeks wore on, the ladies got used to having a goddess among them. They began to share their stories and secrets around me, giggling like girls at times and erupting into full-throated laughter at others.

"How about that handsome new guard?" one chuckled.

"Mmm...mmmm," another replied, making them all titter and roll their eyes.

Or, "The minister's new wife is very beautiful."

"Yes, it's too bad about her teeth." On that, they all bucked out their front teeth by biting their bottom lips, then rolled back onto the divans cackling at their inside joke.

They were a club, a gang, a team. I had never experienced anything like this before. You may know the power of a circle of girlfriends, but I had only ever hung out with the "O"s. Apart from Aunt Demeter, the other goddesses and I didn't really get along. I didn't mind my half-sister Artemis, but like me, she was hardly ever at home. While I was out among the people, she was moving like the wind through the woods, running and leaping with her nymphs and hounds, her silver bow drawn. She wasn't the goddess of the hunt for nothing.

I let myself be pulled into the camaraderie of the Lydian women. It was wonderful to feel a welcome part of a group. As I showed them new ways to stitch and weave, I found myself joining in their storytelling.

"Tell us about your family, Athena," they would prod.

"Is Aphrodite really as beautiful as they say?"

"She is," I answered a little grudgingly. "She's beautiful on the *outside*, anyway."

"Ooooooh," the women snickered.

"Besides, she has a secret weapon. She has a magic girdle that no man can resist."

The women crowded around, their eyes bright with interest.

"She ties it really high, beneath her breasts, so that it lifts them up."

Some of the princesses bounced to their feet, retying their girdles immediately. They clucked with delight at the effect.

"Guys can be so simple," I said. They giggled in agreement, but kept their girdles tied high.

"What about your brothers?" a young one asked. Her name was Arachne. "They're all so handsome, especially Apollo. He must be able to get any girl he wants."

"Not *any*," I said. "The mountain nymph Daphne didn't find him attractive at all. She was so desperate to get away from him that she prayed to be turned into a laurel tree."

"And?" Arachne urged.

"And that's exactly what happened."

The women all fell silent, absorbing this shocking information.

After that, Arachne pulled her loom up next to mine. Whenever I joined the Lydian women, she welcomed me with bright eyes and a smile. She'd launch immediately into questions about where I'd been in my absence. Whom had I seen? What had I done? What was life with the "O"s really like?

We didn't just chatter. When I demonstrated a new stitch, Arachne would bend her whole body forward to watch. A small crease would appear between her arched eyebrows as she memorized exactly what she saw. When she tried the stitch for herself, a dimple would show as she tilted her head and sucked the inside of her cheek in concentration.

"Why do you always have to leave?" she asked one night, as I was winding up some loose threads and tidying up my loom. "Why don't you stay and eat with us?"

I laughed. "I don't eat the same food," I said. "I need my nectar and ambrosia."

"And afterward you could stay the night," Arachne carried on, ignoring me. "We could make you a bed in my room."

"I have my own rooms on Olympus," I said. "They're really wonderful. I have all these shelves and cupboards full of secret compartments. Hephaestus made them for me."

Arachne pushed out her lower lip and furrowed her brow. She picked at her braid as I finished my packing.

Of course I knew better than to think of Arachne as a friend, because we were not equals. I was fond of her, though. I told myself this was only because she was such a good student. The work on her loom became ever more intricate and accurate. Her skill increased with my every visit.

But I had a hunch that Dad would not approve of the current situation. I was also feeling uncomfortable that I'd given away details about

Aphrodite's belt and Apollo's adventures...among other things. The ladies laughed at the stories and then forgot them, but I sensed that Arachne stored them away like treasure.

"You know you can't repeat the things I tell you about Olympus," I said.

"I know," said Arachne. "I'll keep your secrets, because we're friends."

She looked so smug I wanted to say something. The problem was, anything I said would have hurt her badly. I bit my tongue.

Maybe I should have established some distance—stayed away for a while and stopped visiting so frequently. My excuse for carrying on as before was that there was work still to be done. But to be honest, I didn't want to give up my place among the Lydian women.

On my very next visit, Arachne was waiting for me flushed and excited. Her eyes sparkled like gems.

"It's my birthday next week," she said.

"There's going to be a big party. The royalty from neighboring countries have been invited. I've told all the princesses that you'll be there."

I froze. I wanted to go. A royal party sounded like fun to me. I also wanted to make Arachne happy, to see her clap her hands and bounce on her toes, all dimples. But I knew that going to the party would be a really bad idea.

"I'm sorry but I can't come, Arachne."

"Why not?" she asked, her face falling. "You don't even know when it is!"

"It's not that. It's..."

Arachne folded her arms, "It's what?"

"Well, if I came to your party, I'd have to go to everyone else's. As a goddess, I can't be seen to be favoring only Lydia. Right?"

"You're not favoring Lydia, you're favoring me. It's my birthday. I'm your friend."

She stared at me, waiting for my response.

You're not my friend, would have sounded mean. But the fact that she was wrestling with me, trying to impose her will against mine—now I *knew* Dad would not approve.

"I'm really sorry," I said.

This time, I decided to stay away until after Arachne's birthday celebrations, to give her time to cool down. When I visited again, I would ask her how her party went. She'd be excited to tell me because she would have had such a great party anyway. The awkwardness would be forgotten.

I waited almost a month. I was so sure that everything would go according to plan, I hummed a tune to myself as I strolled down the slopes of Mount Olympus to rejoin the Lydian women. In the middle of my music making, I bumped into my half-brother Hermes. He was sitting on a low stone wall at a crossroads, examining the wings of his sandals. It's not usually a good sign to find the messenger god lying in wait for you. I'm sure he must sometimes announce good news, being the divine bearer of both good news and bad—but his messenger bag always seems to carry more news of the bad kind.

"How bad is it?" I asked, sliding onto the wall beside him.

"Dad doesn't know yet," he answered.

Which meant I wouldn't want Dad to know, which meant it was very bad.

I looked him in the eye. "Thanks."

"Arachne has been bragging that she's a better weaver than you are."

I opened my mouth to object.

"It gets worse. She has been showing off a tapestry as proof."

My mouth dropped open again—I couldn't believe the insolence!

"But it gets even worse than that," Hermes interjected before I could begin. "The tapestry is woven with scenes of the gods'..." he coughed, "um...indiscretions."

Everything that was solid—the stone wall, the mountain—fell away, leaving something like motion-sickness in my stomach.

"The tapestry," Hermes continued, putting a hand on each of my shoulders to prop me up, his gaze drilling into my eyes, "is very detailed."

"I understand," I breathed.

"Zeus - does - not - know - yet," my brother slowly repeated.

"I've got it," I said. I gave his arm a squeeze as I leapt off the wall and made like Artemis for Lydia.

On my way there, I battled with my guilt. Hermes had shown me where my loyalties should have been. He'd risked Dad's wrath, the most terrible wrath in the world, by telling me first and not going straight to Zeus. For all their shortcomings, I'm sure Artemis, Apollo, Hephaestus, Dionysus, and even Ares would have done the same thing for me—or for any one of us. My team was Zeus' children, and instead of honoring that, I'd sat around with a bunch of girls I barely knew and gossiped about my brothers and sisters.

Hopping across the Aegean Islands as if they

were stepping stones, I remembered Arachne's sweetness. Surely she wouldn't have betrayed my trust. This must all be one big mistake.

But just in case it wasn't a mistake, when I arrived at the door to the gynaikon I shifted into the shape of an old woman. I hobbled through the room leaning on a cane until I stood next to Arachne, alone at her loom. The weaving was indeed flawless—yet with a twist in my stomach I saw that the pictures so beautifully drawn with her colored threads were all depictions of the stories I'd told her.

"Is this your work, child?" I asked in a reedy voice, like a crone's.

"Yes it is," she confirmed, tossing a long braid proudly over her shoulder and straightening up so I could get a better view of her loom.

"It is beautifully done, but you should be more careful not to offend the gods."

"Why should I care if I do?" she said, tipping up her chin. "I hope *Athena* is offended."

"Why do you say that?" I croaked. I wasn't acting. I felt as if I'd been punched in the stomach.

"Well, for a start, it would serve her right to see that I'm the better weaver."

"That isn't wise," I said, hardly able to stop my own voice from coming through. "You shouldn't say that you're better than a goddess!"

"I'm tired of her coming here and thinking she's so much better than the rest of us," Arachne sniffed. "If she thinks she's so much better, she should compare her weaving to mine. We could have an open competition. She'll see she's not better at everything.

"Look," she said, waving an arm toward the loom beside her where I had left some of my own work. "You can be the judge. Athena's weaving is fabulous, right? The work is so fine you can't even see where one color turns into the next.

"But look at mine," she said turning back to her own loom. "My work is as perfect as hers is, plus mine's original. Look at the scenes. I guarantee you'll see things you've never seen before!" She laughed. She was laughing at my family—she was laughing at the gods.

Anger rose in me like a head of steam and I felt my shape shifting. The bent crone straightened, rising up into my usual human form. Terror and recognition flashed in Arachne's eyes, but I kept morphing. I grew larger, more powerful, brighter, filling the room. My head and shoulders now pressed against the high ceiling. In one movement I shredded the tapestry from the loom.

Arachne, all bravado gone, watched me growing like a mushroom cloud above her, her eyes and mouth round with terror. Panicking, she scrambled across the room and threw a scarf over a beam.

Was she about to hang herself?! This was all going horribly wrong. Immediately, I zapped Arachne into a spider—her scarf turned into her thread. I watched her climb up it to safety. She rested when she reached the beam, her thorax and abdomen heaving, her eight legs trembling.

I shifted back into my usual human form. We regarded each other silently.

The question was, what should I do now? If I turned her back into a human, I knew The Twelve (well, eleven) would not consider her punished. A good scare—and it must have been good, if she feared my wrath more than death—would not make up for her being so disrespectful. Mortals were mortals and gods were gods, and Zeus would be determined to set an example to avoid any further confusion.

I decided the best thing to do would be to leave Arachne as a spider and let that be her punishment.

"I'm so sorry, Arachne," I said. "You really should have known better than to mock the gods. They really don't like that." As some consolation, I gave her the ability to weave webs more beautiful and intricate than any tapestry.

If you're worried that I didn't have to pay for

my part in this, don't worry. As you'll soon see, I paid in guilt and embarrassment. I have also had to suffer through millennia of this story being told as if I turned Arachne into a spider just because I was jealous. This might not seem like a big deal to you, but to me it's almost insufferable. It implies that Arachne was the better weaver, and that she would have won the competition.

I—AM—THE—GODDESS—OF—WEAVING. Come on, people!

A Lesson

I stayed away from Earth for a while after that. Humans had turned out to be surprisingly dangerous creatures. On Olympus, I was ashamed of myself before the other gods and goddesses, so I avoided them too. I kept to my rooms.

The story about Arachne and her tapestry, of course, leaked out. Everyone knew that to feel part of the "in" crowd with the Lydian women, I'd blabbed about some private details behind my family's back. Luckily, with the tapestry destroyed, nobody knew exactly what I'd blabbed. So, instead of taking things personally, the gods and goddesses were just generally scornful. Every time I heard a giggle in the corridor, I was sure they were laughing at me.

The spider punishment worked. From what I

could tell, Dad thought both the Lydians and I had learned our lessons. He didn't give me a lecture or throw a lightning bolt at the Lydian palace. He didn't really do anything at all, except leave me to myself for a couple of weeks and then stick me with extra duties. He made me stand by his throne all day. Only now and then would he ask my opinion. This was his way of forcing me out of my rooms to face the consequences of my actions. Dad can be sly like that.

My great-grandmother Gaia felt sorry for me. She gave me a chaperon for the exile I imposed on myself every night: a pet snake. I appreciated Gaia's gesture, and the snake was the perfect companion. He didn't demand much attention, just a mouse once in a while, so I was free to keep brooding. I named him Erichthonius—Thonius, for short. That should have been the entire story. But it wasn't.

Hephaestus, the most left-out of all the gods, also felt sorry for me. He knocked on my door, carrying one of his inventions.

"This," he said, setting down his contraption, "is especially useful when you're moping."

It was a golden coffee table with three legs, set on wheels. I looked up at Hephaestus from where I lay sprawled on my couch. "I am not moping," I said.

"This table will bring you whatever you ask," he continued.

"Bring us some food!" he commanded. With a slight squeaking, the table wheeled itself out of the room. Hephaestus smiled at me, at a loss for conversation. He didn't really know what to do with me now that he found me in my black funk. His face brightened when we heard the squeak of the table returning. As promised, it was laden with a jug of nectar and cakes of ambrosia, as well as cheeses, olives, and fruit.

"Come on, Athena," he said, sitting down on the couch opposite me. "You have to eat something." He helped himself to a few grapes. "They're very sweet," he said, handing me a bunch.

I took the grapes. I appreciated his kindness.

After that, Hephaestus came regularly to visit. He would send the table out to get us some food, and then we'd dine together discussing the latest project he was working on. It was always something so clever that I couldn't help but ask questions. Hephaestus was not just a cunning craftsman; he'd found a way to draw me out of myself without having to talk about the real issues.

One night he turned up looking smug. "I've made a new set of armor," he announced.

I raised an eyebrow from my usual position on the couch.

"Actually," he corrected himself, standing up a little taller for emphasis, "I've made a new metal."

He had my attention now.

"Think of it as a fluid," he said, his hands shaping flowing curves before him. "When the wearer puts the armor on, it flows over her body and moves with her, like a second skin."

He looked me in the eye, to make sure I was

ready for the best part. "But it doesn't behave like a liquid when it's struck. It's stronger than bronze. It's even stronger than iron. It's stronger than any metal we've seen before."

"No!" I couldn't help exclaiming. "Wait," I said. "You said 'when it flows over *her* body...'"

He gave me a wolfish grin.

"I made the prototype for a woman," he confirmed. "I made it for you."

"I have to see it!" I said, sitting up.

He bowed and made an elaborate sweep with his arm toward my door. "As you wish, madam," he said.

Well, I had to break my self-imposed exile after that. We emerged from my rooms, surprising a few gods in the corridors.

Hidden in his workshop, deep in the caves of Lemnos, the armor really was everything that Hephaestus had described, except he'd forgotten to mention its beauty. The new metal was a lovely pale blue, exactly the color of the sea when the sun has just started to set.

"Can I try it on?" I asked. Unlike the other goddesses, I'd never been very interested in clothes or jewelry. This was different. This armor gave me butterflies.

"Of course," Hephaestus said, pointing to a screen that I could change behind.

I hurried toward it with the armor, discarding items of clothing in my haste. A sandal here. A sandal there. My *cuirass*. My girdle. I emerged with my new armor on. It fit me like a glove. I felt as bright and luminous as the lovely new metal. I felt born again.

Within days, a horrible story began to spread that Hephaestus had fathered a baby when I followed him to his workshop. Nobody went so far as to actually accuse me of being the mother, which is a good thing, because I would have borrowed one of Dad's lightning bolts and done some real damage—but let's just say that I was implicated. According to the rumors, the baby was my pet snake, Thonius. Only, in the stories, Thonius wasn't a real snake, he was half snake and half human. Or, in some stories, he was a human baby, found wrapped in the coils of a great serpent.

All of the versions made absolutely no sense. Why weren't people smart enough to see how stupid these rumors were? How could I stop these lies from spreading and growing? I felt like setting all the gossips straight—but of course I couldn't. There was no single source. Besides, a goddess making a fuss just looked guilty.

I felt terrible for Hephaestus. He was brave enough to visit me one last time.

"I'm really sorry," I said.

"You didn't do anything," he replied.

"I wonder who did. It's all so idiotic. The stories don't even add up or make sense! Who could have started them?"

"You really can't imagine?" he said.

"No. Who?"

"Maybe someone wants you to learn a lesson

about feeding gossip mills."

I felt really guilty then.

"Don't worry, Athena. It will all blow over eventually. Until then, it's probably best if I don't visit for a while. I just wanted to tell you myself, so you don't think there are any hard feelings, because there are not. I've lived through worse mischief than this," he shrugged.

I had a much harder time than Hephaestus did shrugging the malice away. I tried to ignore all the insane gossip, knowing it would eventually die down; but I also knew that the effects of the stories could never be undone. A rumor once out there does its damage and leaves its mark.

If someone really was trying to teach me a lesson, he or she succeeded. I was now painfully aware of how careless and irresponsible I'd been in gossiping with the Lydian women. I was powerful enough to destroy the evidence, and to turn the key witness into a spider, but these new rumors showed me what a destructive force I'd been playing with. A few ill-considered words can literally change lives.

Plus, even worse than the gossip, was all the tittering. There wasn't a single immortal who really believed the rumor, but that didn't prevent them from being amused by it. Every nymph and nereid who visited Olympus found a reason to hang out in the hallway outside my rooms. They swallowed their sniggers the moment I opened my door, but went back to their irritating giggles once I closed it. I even heard a few of them whispering below my windows late one night. Whenever I appeared in court, instead of paying any attention to the proceedings, the defendants and plaintiffs turned to stare at me. They whispered in each other's ears, all animosity between them forgotten. I stopped turning up to stand beside Dad's throne.

Dad was worried—worried enough to blunder down the corridors to my rooms, preceded by a chorus of squeals as he unceremoniously opened a string of wrong doors. When he finally found me, he paced about looking at my snake with distaste.

"It's not his fault," I reminded Dad.

"I know. It's got nothing to do with him. I just don't understand the attraction," he grumbled. "How can a slimy thing make a good pet?"

"Snakes aren't slimy," I said. "You're the omniscient king of the gods. You're supposed to know that."

Dad shrugged, "He's not warm and fuzzy though, is he?"

"No," I agreed, sliding my fingers along Thonius' cool black scales.

"Cuddling up to him is only going to make you morose," Dad said. "You're going to start wearing lots of black makeup or something. He'll encourage your moping, when what you need to do is come out, go about your business, and show everyone that they're being stupid and you don't care!"

I didn't answer. I kept stubbornly stroking my pet snake.

My Boys

That night after Dad left, I gathered up Thonius and Hephaestus' magic table, and went down to the Acropolis in Athens. I guess I was running away; although, that's not how I saw it at the time.

I had not visited Athens in a while. The hilltop was quiet. A wind bent the tufts of grass that pushed up between the paving stones. The temples loomed silent, their columns warmed by the flickering light of fires within—fires that had been lit for me. Through all of the hullabaloo over Arachne and Hephaestus and Thonius, the Athenians had sent me love and prayers from these temples. Athens, I decided, would now be home.

Thonius seemed content. The temple altars were perfect for basking on. There were plenty of mice to catch. As for me, with Hephaestus' handy gift, I could summon anything I wanted, including all the nectar and ambrosia I might need. And who needed the "O"s when the mortals were so much more inclusive? The Athenians quickly grew to love Thonius, the sacred snake who had come to guard my temple. They made a ritual of feeding him, and saw bad omens if he failed to appear. We settled in.

It was a little lonely at first. I hadn't realized how comforting it was to be surrounded by the "O"s even when I wasn't speaking to them. Eventually, like Artemis who had her woodland nymphs, I found new companions, the Greek heroes. You may have heard of them because their names have come down through the ages: Heracles, Perseus, Jason. They all faced impossible challenges—the slaying of monsters like the Nemean Lion or the Gorgon Medusa, or the capture of the Golden Fleece—and if there's one thing I like, it's a challenge. I love riddles, puzzles, that ancient game you now call backgammon, anything where the best solution is not obvious and you have to work it out. I offered my help to these heroes, and they gratefully accepted it. We had thrilling adventures together and enjoyed each other's company. My new friends never forgot that I was a goddess, and best of all, they were much too busy for gossip.

I took good care of them. I was the one who guided Perseus to the serpent-crowned Medusa. Looking into that Gorgon's eyes would turn you into stone. We picked our way between the grotesque rocks that guarded her cave—the stony remains of past visitors. For months, I had trained Perseus to fight while looking only at the reflections in his bronze shield, so he would not have to meet Medusa's deadly gaze himself. At the critical moment, when he raised his sword against her, I steadied his arm with my hand, giving him the confidence to strike off her head with one blow. Medusa's snake-hair writhed and hissed as her severed head fell.

But there's a limit to the protection I can give. The downside to having humans as friends is that you can't save them from everything. They are mortal and you are not. On any day, Fate can come knocking and one of them will be gone.

I was with Jason on his last night alive. We were on the beach. He sat with his back rounded against the rotten timbers of his famous ship, the Argo. It had been pulled up onto the sands and dedicated to Poseidon years ago, and now it sagged with neglect.

Jason looked out with unseeing eyes, blind to the moonlight on the sea. He had become one of those old men whose sight turns inward, who spends all his time reviewing his days of glory, polishing memories into a stone within his chest.

"Do you remember designing the Argo together?" he said.

I wouldn't have quite used the word *together*. Many years ago, I stood with him on wet sand, only a few feet from where we sat now, and carefully drew out my design for the ship with a sharpened stick.

"Yes," I answered.

"Do you remember how I was debating which of Greece's men deserved to become the fifty Argonauts—my companions in the search for the Golden Fleece—and you surprised me by recommending a woman?"

"Yes," I smiled. "Atalanta of Calydon, the virgin huntress. You did well to take my advice. She turned out to be one of your best warriors—and she helped keep you all well fed."

"When you first put forward her name, you and I were standing in the sea, skimming stones down the bright path laid by a rising moon. I thought, even if I never find the Golden Fleece, I'm skimming stones with a goddess."

He turned his eyes to me, "You've been a good friend, Athena."

Behind us, the great ship shuddered. There

was a groan of over-tired timbers, and a snapping like the breaking of twigs. Then, the whole ship disintegrated on top of my friend, creating an instant burial mound.

Fate had walked by.

It's hard, even as a goddess, to keep sustaining such losses. I may be immortal, but I'm far from unfeeling. Unfortunately, it is also impossible to stop myself from forming new bonds. With the "O"s, as with humans, you can't choose if and whom you'll love.

So, even as I mourned Jason and watched him fade from my lively companion into a distant legend, I made new friends. There was Diomedes, who stood head and shoulders above other men. I'm not saying that just as a figure of speech. He really was unusually tall and strong. All the "O"s can shape-shift, but there are some shapes that come more naturally to us, and the human form in which I normally walk on Earth is not what you might call dainty. It was nice to have a friend even taller and stronger than I was. Besides, Diomedes was quiet. He didn't say much, but whenever he spoke you could tell he had been listening. As the goddess of wisdom—and one often ignored on Olympus—I liked that.

Another good friend I loved for the opposite reason. You couldn't shut Odysseus up. He was full of ideas and wry observations, witty jokes and funny asides, always cutting deals and trying out new schemes—constantly cracking me up. He had a mind like Hephaestus' new metal: bright and fluid, able to split and run along many channels at once; yet also able to solidify, to focus, to be still and concentrated. Of all my friends, Odysseus was most like me.

However, my favorite at that time was a demigod, Achilles. He was the son of the sea nymph Thetis, and Peleus, King of Myrmidon. He was also the greatest warrior alive. You'd think with this reputation, the body to go with it, and his soft blond curls (as pretty as Aphrodite's), he would be in the middle of a crowd of admiring sidekicks and groupies making goo-goo eyes. But Achilles kept himself to himself.

I would often meet him at his favorite spot on the riverbank. I always made sure I was a little late, so that I could approach unobserved and watch him as he stared moodily down into the meandering water. He was so perfect, it was a pleasure just to look at him. He was a work of art, a Greek statue come to life.

"You know, I was dipped into a river like this once," he said one day.

"Hardly like this," I answered. "You were dipped into the dark waters of the River Styx, which separates this world from the next."

He looked at me ruefully. Well, of course I would know.

"Your mother was trying to make you immortal, but she forgot that she was holding you by your right heel. She left a little mortal patch."

His face slowly melted into a reluctant grin.

"I've never heard it described that way before," he said, looking down at his right foot.

"It's very odd to know exactly through which point death will claim you," he said. "It's very odd to know that you will die at all."

There was no fear in his voice. Many men are afraid of death, but that wasn't troubling Achilles. As he turned his gaze back to me, he only looked puzzled by his mortality. He was an immortal trapped in a mortal's body, shackled by a ring of skin around his right ankle.

More and more I felt like a mortal trapped in an immortal's life, forming mortal bonds and then having to live on and watch my loved ones die.

Below us, the water idly sucked on stones.

I reached out my fingers. He closed his hand firmly around mine.

A Feathered Friend

Between teaching Diomedes how to make his spear lethal with his strength and reach, and sparring with Achilles so that his sword moved as swiftly as thought, and helping Odysseus with a dozen schemes, my days were full. Plus, there were festivals given in my honor, new temples built and dedicated to me, wishes to grant, and prayers to answer. In the quiet of night after a busy day, I would loop Thonius around my shoulders and walk out onto the rocky terrace of the Acropolis. As I looked down at Athens, the darkness broken only by the flicker of a few candles in windows, or by a torch making its way through the streets, I would listen to the sleeping breath of my people and feel tender, protective. But despite feeling welcome and purposeful—needed even—I missed my family.

I missed the gods. I missed being part of an "us." Here, loved and admired as I was, I was always one of "them."

Most of all, I missed my father. There had been no sign from Dad since I ran away—because looking back, running away was what I'd done. Dad was right. I had not faced the consequences of my actions. I had only removed myself from the situation. To my surprise, he had not come begging or blustering that I should go home. He had not sent Hermes to summon me. *Maybe*, I thought, *I've been forgotten.* I was the latecomer to the table, only loosely attached to the rest of The Twelve who were all bound by closer ties of kinship. For all I knew, I might have already been replaced.

Then one night, as I was putting Thonius to bed in his favorite spot on the altar, I heard a fluttering in a far corner of my temple. When I went to look for its source, I found a pair of round yellow eyes staring at me. A little owl was perched on a lip of marble, up among the column tops. I'd often seen his kind flitting around the Acropolis, carrying the remains of some small animal back to clefts in the cliff walls.

"Hello," I said.

He frowned in response. The tufts of white feathers above his eyes gave him an exaggerated scowl. We looked at each other briefly before he hopped and flapped to another column. I followed him. Bit by bit he led me toward the door of the temple. As I put my foot on its worn threshold, he flew down onto my shoulder.

His weight landing upon me, the gentle scratch of his talons as he shifted around to find the perfect perch, his body heat warming my ear, all made me happy.

"Where do you want to go?" I asked him.

He blinked his yellow eyes determinedly in one direction. I turned to face him another way, but he simply rotated his head to keep his original focus. He blinked toward Mount Olympus.

I sighed. Home had been niggling at my mind.

"It's time to face the music, whatever the tune," I said to the little owl.

He puffed up his feathers for a moment in approval. It looked like an *it'll be OK* shrug.

"But if I'm going, you're going too," I said.

The little owl puffed his feathers again.

So I wore him to dinner like a new brooch.

"Excuse me, but you have a hump on your shoulder," Ares chortled, as if he'd just seen me that morning. "Has it got a name?"

"Glaux," I said, naming him with the Ancient Greek word for owl.

"Your owl is called Owl?" Ares scoffed. "I thought you were supposed to be clever?"

"I'm not sure you should be bringing him to dinner," said Mrs. O, as displeased by my feathered friend as by my own reappearance. "Imagine if we all started bringing our pets."

"He's not bothering anyone," Dad said without looking over. He poured himself and U.P. two great goblets of nectar. "It's not as if your peacocks don't make a nuisance of themselves, dropping their feathers all over the palace and the lawns."

Dad had not greeted me when I'd entered the dining hall, or addressed me when I'd pulled out my chair. He behaved as if there were nothing worthy of comment going on—as if I were only where I should be. And maybe I was.

"Oh yes, those stupid peacocks. They'd make good feather dusters," Ares laughed. "And what about Apollo's crows? Caaaaaw! Caaaaaw!" he croaked, tucking his thumbs into his armpits and flapping his elbows. "It's enough to drive you nuts in the morning."

Apollo arched a brow, "Maybe it's the only way to get you out of bed?"

"Or Aphrodite's swans," Ares went on, paying Apollo no attention.

"How can you possibly object to swans?" Aphrodite giggled.

"They're beautiful but very bad tempered, like someone I know," teased Ares.

Hephaestus, meanwhile, had taken his seat beside me and was examining Glaux intently. "Did you notice how his lower eyelids close up as much as his upper eyelids close down?" he asked me, one craft god to another.

"Maybe we should ask the kitchen for some raw meat for him," suggested Aunt Demeter.

"He can stay," said Mrs. O disdainfully. "But it doesn't mean we have to feed him."

Apollo tore a small strip off the meat on his plate and handed it to me.

"Thanks, Apollo," I said.

My brother winked, then turned his attention back to his twin. Artemis flashed me a smile before they resumed their conversation.

I realized that around this table there were three kinds of people. There were those who were happy to see me—Hephaestus who had by now taken the meat from me and was using it to tempt Glaux onto his own shoulder; Dad who was making sure nobody gave me a hard time even though he himself was ignoring me; Aunt Demeter who was busy picking out choice morsels for my plate again; and even Ares, so quick to include me in his jovial world. There were those who didn't particularly like my presence—Mrs. O for one and U.P. for another. And then there were the majority who had no strong feelings either way. If you conducted the same survey for any one of us, you'd get about the same result. It finally dawned on me that this is just how a big family works. None of the "O"s, I now realized, doubted for a second that I had the right to be there. I was one of The Twelve. The only one who hadn't seen that I belonged here was me.

The family joked and bickered through dinner, and I joined in the laughter and teasing as I'd never done before. Nobody mentioned my absence or asked about my reappearance. I noticed Glaux staring quite fixedly at Dad on more than one occasion. I knew Dad had sent my new friend to me. It warmed me to think that the great god

Zeus had gone to the trouble of finding such a gentle way to coax me home, instead of summoning me as he could have. It was good to feel part of the family again—and I was surprised how quickly things returned to normal once I let them. We might even have stayed in relative harmony, if it wasn't for that stupid apple.

The Bomb

The small, bouncing apple, made of polished gold, thumped down the center of the table, its unusual density sending the plates airborne with each impact, boomf, boomf, boomf. It rolled to a stop in front of Zeus, coming to rest inscription-side up. *For the fairest,* it glinted seductively.

It had literally dropped out of thin air. I glanced at the smith god. Barely perceptibly, Hephaestus shook his head.

"What does it say?" several voices asked, although we'd all somehow managed to read it from our odd angles.

For the fairest.

There was a pause, and then three hands reached to claim it.

Mrs. O was Hand Number One. No surprise;

she's famous for her flawless white skin. "Hera of the alabaster arms," you'll sometimes hear her called, or "the white-armed goddess." That milky skin is part of her great pride. It's hard to stay alabaster-white in the Ancient Greek World. It's soaked in sunshine. You'd have to remain indoors all the time. No working in the fields. No standing in doorways, minding shops or taverns. No shopping in markets or running errands in the streets. Fairness marks you out as a lady of leisure, a wealthy woman who has others to do such things for you. It's seen as a sign of beauty for this reason—including here on Olympus.

Hand Number Two, predictably, belonged to Aphrodite. She laughed her musical laugh as if happily surprised that there were others claiming the apple. But her face collapsed into a pout when those other claims weren't immediately withdrawn.

"How rude!" she exclaimed, wrinkling her pretty nose. After all, she was the goddess of love and beauty. "The fairest," to her, meant the most beautiful and not just the palest. Which meant *her*, or so she thought. (I didn't agree. I found Hera's beauty much more interesting.)

The biggest surprise though, certainly to myself, was that Hand Number Three was my own. Don't get me wrong. This is not false modesty. I know I'm attractive. When people call me "bright eyed," they mean it as a compliment. But I wasn't reaching out because I thought myself as pretty as Aphrodite or as alluring as Hera. Nor had I read "fairest" to mean the most just—even though that would, in fact, have been me. (I sometimes feel as if I'm the only one on Olympus who stops to think about whether anything is fair at all.) To tell you the truth, I had reached out instinctively with the curiosity a craft god feels toward something that has been uniquely crafted. Then, once I'd reached out my hand, something strange happened.

Instead of hooting and teasing me, Ares, with his love for conflict, licked his lips at the even match. Hephaestus also looked pleased. For once his spoiled wife wasn't going to automatically get her own way. Dad narrowed his eyes as if looking at me from a great distance and stroked his chin to hide a small smile of pride. To him, I realized, I was the most beautiful of the three. Of course, every father thinks that. He made me.

I'd never thought of myself as a beauty before. It felt good. Besides, withdrawing my hand now and saying "Oh, I just wanted to take a look at that apple" would have sounded lame.

"Zeus?" Aphrodite whined.

"Zeus!" Mrs. O demanded.

I gave Dad a half smile. The situation was very awkward.

"Oh bother!" grumbled Dad. He picked up the apple and examined it. "Maybe it should go to Apollo?" he joked.

Hera and Aphrodite glared at him. This contest was no joking matter.

Dad's eyes wandered from me to U.P., then brightened. He threw the apple to Hermes, who caught it with a practiced hand and slipped it into his messenger bag.

"Go find them a judge," Zeus directed. "And while you're at it, have the stables prepare my chariot. I'm going for a drive."

~~~

Soon, Hermes was leading Hera, Aphrodite, and me nimbly down a mountain, his feet in their winged sandals striding with purpose and determination. I was pleased to see that olive groves cloaked the foothills. On a grassy crest, lolling on a boulder, was Hermes' target: a handsome young man keeping a lazy eye on his cattle. His name was Paris, and he was the youngest son of King Priam of Troy. He didn't get to his feet to greet us, but remained as he was, propped up on an elbow.

Hermes knew exactly what he was doing when he chose this princeling. You need a certain arrogance to not even straighten your clothes when being approached by the gods—the same arrogance you need to play judge between three goddesses.
~~~

Hermes showed Paris the apple. In very few words he explained the situation, ending with, "Zeus commands that you judge which of these goddesses is the fairest."

To his credit, Paris did try a diplomatic solution. He offered to split the apple into three. Hera scowled and Aphrodite shook her golden curls in answer.

"Very well," said Paris. "Step up and be judged one at a time."

Hera approached the boulder. She raised her graceful arms above her head to show off her fabulous figure. "If you pick me," she said, turning her body around before Paris, letting him see her curves from all angles, "I'll make you the most powerful man on the planet."

The Trojan prince gave her a roguish grin. "I can't be bribed," he said.

I went next. I stood before him as stiff as a board, grumpy at the unwelcome scrutiny.

"If you pick me I'll give you victory in war,

and *wisdom*—which you obviously need. You know even Zeus didn't dare choose between us, don't you?"

"I'm not a soldier," he answered, matter-of-fact. "And the wisest thing now is to judge this as fairly as I can."

I blushed.

Then it was Aphrodite's turn. She walked slowly toward him, holding his gaze as her hips swung below her like a pendulum. She bent over him so that her hair tumbled down, grazing his cheek, enveloping him in its smell. With two perfect white teeth, she bit her lower lip, as if it took great self-control not to kiss him. Then she breathed, "Give me that apple, and I will give you the most beautiful woman in the world."

Paris looked at her as if from the bottom of a well whose warm waters slowed all thought and sound.

She held out her hand.

He placed the apple in it.

So much for being immune to bribery.

Fine Print

Paris had to wait to get his reward. They say you should always read the fine print, and that goes doubly if you're making a deal with the wily Aphrodite. Who knows if Paris heard and really understood the catch in the word "woman." With Aphrodite leaning over him, filling his senses, I have little doubt which woman was on his mind. But of course, Aphrodite, strictly speaking, is not a woman. So with her golden apple in her hand, the goddess slipped away.

Any disappointment Paris felt was short-lived. After all, the most beautiful mortal woman in the world isn't bad for a consolation prize. And the most beautiful woman at that time was Helen. She was one of those illegitimate children of Dad's who made Mrs. O so unhappy. It was said Helen was unusually fine and delicate because her mother was a swan. As she grew into womanhood, Helen was so desirable that all the princes of Greece became her suitors. Now she was married to one of the most powerful kings of them all, Menelaus of Sparta. How was Aphrodite going to give Helen to Paris, a little princeling from the city of Troy, far on the other side of the sea?

I woke one morning to find all of Olympus in an uproar.

"Helen has run away with Paris!" Ares yelled gleefully across the room when I appeared for breakfast. He leaned forward over the table as I pulled out my chair, eager to catch me up on developments. Around us, every member of the family was quarreling.

"Paris found an excuse to visit Sparta. Aphrodite sent a breeze to hurry his ships along. He was a guest at the Spartan palace for nine days. Nine days of making eyes at Helen, right under Menelaus' nose. Then yesterday Menelaus was called away to a funeral. Last night, the two slipped onto one of Paris' ships and sailed away!"

Aphrodite sat with her arms folded, the pink rose petal of her lower lip fully budded out. "You can't say I forced her into anything," she said.

Mrs. O, usually so calm and cold, was ablaze. She was on her feet, pacing in front of Aphrodite. She took this incident as a triple insult. She was the goddess of marriage and a very high profile marriage had been violated. Even more offensive to Mrs. O, one of the violators was none other than the lowly cowherd (royal or not) who had declared her inferior to Aphrodite. And, to heap insult on injury, his partner in crime was one of the hated offspring of her husband's numerous infidelities.

"This is ridiculous," I said to Aphrodite. "Tell Paris to bring Helen back. He can't go kidnapping the Queen of Sparta on a whim."

"It wasn't a whim, and it wasn't a kidnapping. Helen's been waiting for a chance to get out of her marriage," Aphrodite said, sticking another knife into Mrs. O. “She didn’t steal away in the night with just the clothes on her back. She took nearly all the palace treasures and five serving women. She was prepared!”

“She took gold from my temple,” Apollo said calmly. Two little lines in the corners of his mouth were the only signs of his displeasure.

Aphrodite shrugged. That was no concern of hers.

“She left behind a child, a girl of nine,” said Aunt Demeter.

Aphrodite shrugged again.

“My point is that she wanted to run away. She’s been dreaming about it. She already had plans, ready to hatch, in her head. All I did was give her the Trojan prince to run away with and send winds to help him find her.”

“Two can play at that game,” stormed Mrs. O, turning on her heel. And when I say “stormed”—she sent a cold and bitter tempest against Paris and Helen’s ships, which didn’t succeed in sinking them but tossed them about like plastic snow in a snow globe. The resulting seasickness would have been enough to cool any passion. In the meantime, Mrs. O sent word to Menelaus.

The Spartan king immediately rode across Greece, rallying every leader, prince, and king to take up the fight. "If this outrage goes unpunished," he thundered, "what is to keep your wives safe by your sides? Any stranger could walk in and take them. And the Trojan didn't just take my wife! He stole away with all my gold and silver. Who will extend hospitality again when any guest can help himself to all his host's possessions?"

Menelaus soon had all the kings of Greece convinced that Paris had trespassed not only against him, but also against each of them.

Across the land, the villages rang with the sound of hammers striking metal, reinforcing shields, fashioning spears and swords. The forests were filled with the creak and groan of trees being felled to make masts for warships. Cows bellowed and pigs squealed as they were slaughtered to provide salted meat for soldiers and sailors. The air smelled of burnt hair as hides were singed to make leather.

I was outraged by Aphrodite's handiwork. She couldn't have cared less. The only other person not appalled by these developments was Ares.

"War," he said, rubbing his hands together. "A really big juicy war..."

War

Not even Zeus could have guessed just how "big and juicy" the Trojan War would get. It dragged on in fits and starts for nine years. Then, it got even worse—because one by one, we got involved. Starting with—of all the gods—Apollo.

In the tenth year of the fighting, the daughter of Apollo's Trojan priest was taken captive by the leader of the Greek forces, King Agamemnon. That night, as we sat down to dinner on Olympus, the priest crossed the sands between the Trojan walls and the Greek ships, which had all been drawn up on the beach. He moved slowly, clutching the ransom he had come to offer for his daughter and leaning on a staff. It was the staff of Apollo, and wound about it were the sacred emblems of the archer god. In the fitful firelight from the Greek camp, those emblems winked gold. They were the old man's only protection from the Greek sentries who stood nervously watching his approach.

The old man was taken deep into the belly of a ship. Thirty of the Greeks' finest fighting men were gathered around a wooden table. They were still stained with the blood and sweat of battle. The air was heavy with their musk.

"What do you want, old man?" Agamemnon snarled from the head of the table.

A few of the men laughed, but others looked away, uncomfortable at such rudeness being shown to a priest. Only Diomedes stood up respectfully.

The old man hobbled forward and laid his bundle on top of the maps spread open on the table. "I have come for my daughter," he said. He drew back the tattered cloth sack to reveal a mound of gleaming treasure.

"I think this is a very fair ransom," said Diomedes. The priest peered up at him thankfully.

The rest of the group murmured in agreement. "It's a fair ransom."

"I have no use for your baubles!" bellowed Agamemnon.

There was a shocked silence.

The king wiped spittle from his mouth with the back of his hand. "But I can always use a slave girl. I am not giving back your daughter."

Like a current moving through the room, the men tensed. The priest hoped they would speak out for him. Instead, Agamemnon spat into the dust on the floor.

"Now get out of here," the king said. "Before I take you for a slave as well!"

The sentries watched the priest struggling back across the sand. He was more bent now than when he had come. Before he reached Troy's gates he stopped and straightened. Leaning hard on Apollo's staff he arched his back to face the heavens. Letting his tears flow, he called out to his master, "Hear me, Apollo, God of the Silver Bow! If ever I have pleased you, pay back these Greeks—your arrows for my tears!"

Up in the lofty halls of Olympus, my golden brother, usually so remote in his beauty, so loathe to pay attention to the imperfect worldly din, rose from the table with such abruptness that his chair cartwheeled backward. We all fell silent. You could hear his silver arrows clinking in the quiver on his back. He trembled with indignation that his priest had been so slighted.

Hera opened her mouth to stop him, but with one sweep Apollo shouldered his great bow and strode out of the hall. Before he had even reached the doorway, my brother had fitted a shaft to the string. For nine days he loosed his arrows at the Greeks, striking them with plague, killing not just the men but their dogs, their mules, their horses, so that the whole camp was strewn with reeking corpses and the sand was sticky with blood.

Hera could not just sit by watching the Greeks die like ants under Apollo's rain of arrows.

After all, the Greeks were fighting to punish the violation of a marriage, and she was the goddess of marriage. In Hera's mind at least, the Greeks were fighting for her.

I could not just sit by either. Diomedes, Odysseus, and Achilles had not yet been struck down by Apollo, but that was only a matter of luck. My brother was firing without discrimination. Any Greek was a fair target.

To my surprise, Hera approached me with a plan. Together, we slipped down to Achilles' ship and prodded him to gather a council. We told him that Apollo had sent the plague, and to end it the Greeks would have to placate the archer god.

The Greek leaders gathered once again in the belly of Agamemnon's ship. I slipped in unseen among them. This time, the smell of men was overpowered by that of herbs being burned to ward off illness.

"The priest's daughter has to be returned," Achilles said.

"Why should we return a Trojan woman when they still haven't returned ours?" sneered Agamemnon. By "ours" he meant Helen who was still snuggled up with Paris after all these years, safe inside Troy's walls.

"Apollo is furious at your high-handed treatment of his priest. He is killing us even in the shelter of our ships. We will have traveled half the world to die, not with honor on the battlefield, but like vermin in a hole. You must return his priest's daughter."

Agamemnon folded his arms, each as thick as a man's leg. He didn't like being told what to do, especially not by this pretty boy. Yet he could sense that the rest of the men were behind Achilles. There was not one among them who had not lost some of his best warriors to Apollo's fury.

"I will give the slave girl back," Agamemnon said at last. "But only if she's replaced by another." He turned to Achilles. "By one belonging to you."

Achilles' sword arm twitched as he imagined

cutting the arrogant king in two. I reached out and gave one of his golden locks a tug. He knew it was me, although I remained hidden from the others.

"Don't do it," I whispered in his ear. "Let it go. He might deserve to die, but killing Agamemnon would leave the Greek army in disarray."

Achilles silently sheathed his sword. I made the mistake of thinking that I'd talked some sense into him. Then I made an even bigger mistake: I left.

In the months to come, I would think back on this moment again and again, tormenting myself with what might have happened if I'd just stayed with Achilles a little longer. With me there, I'm sure he would have swallowed Agamemnon's insult. He and Agamemnon would have exchanged women. Achilles would have returned the girl to the priest. In private, Odysseus would have consoled Achilles with a joke about Agamemnon's ego. Apollo would have put down his bow and the rest of the "O"s would have stayed out of it.

But I left. As soon as I was gone, Achilles turned to Agamemnon.

"You," he spat. "Your greed makes you no better than a dog. This is the respect you show your best warrior? I won't fight under you. I'll sit in my ships and watch you drink the poison that you yourself have brewed."

Thus began a sulk that endangered all the Greeks. I pleaded with Achilles. I begged him to swallow his pride for the sake of his men, his friends, and *my* friends Diomedes and Odysseus, who were all in greater danger without him. I tried logic. I tried charm. I cajoled. I even cursed. Achilles wasn't budging.

To make things even worse, Achilles' mother, the sea nymph Thetis, came slipping up Olympus' marble steps, leaving telltale puddles that turned the white-armed goddess, Hera, even paler. Thetis had come to see Big Daddy-O who had loved her when they were young. Kneeling before him, she wrapped one arm around his knees, and reached up with the other to cradle his familiar face in her hand.

"Help the Trojans," she said. "Help them push the Greeks back to their ships and pin them there, trapped between sword and sea. Make them feel the absence of my son, so that they truly regret offending him."

After all those years, the only change that Dad could see in that upturned face was the sadness gathered around her eyes. It made her even lovelier. But he remained silent.

"Answer me, Zeus," she said. "Just say yes or no. You have nothing to fear—although a 'no' would leave me the most dishonored of goddesses, not even able to punish an insult to my son."

"I have plenty to fear," he answered. "What you ask will lead to disaster. You will be driving me into war against my wife, Hera."

Thetis continued to look at him.

With a sigh that rumbled like distant thunder, Dad nodded—and the war got worse.

Not only was Zeus now pitched against Hera, the other Olympians soon joined in and we were pitched god against god. As for me, I was pitched against myself.

My three best friends were fighting on the Greek side, but Troy was one of my cities. Behind her walls, in a citadel, was a statue of me called the Palladium. Every morning the Trojans wreathed it with flowers and poured fresh offerings of wine before it. They thanked me that their city was still standing. But increasingly, my loyalties were divided.

The tallest and strongest man on the field, Diomedes was under constant attack. When he shook from exhaustion, I guided his spear, steadied his aim. When he could hardly stand, I threw the weight of my thrust behind his, helped him drive his sword into his enemy. That enemy was always a Trojan boy whose mother was praying to me. The thought plagued me—plagues me still—but Diomedes was my friend.

Achilles, once he finally returned to the fray, also drew a lot of enemy attention. The Trojans would set upon him in packs. I jumped up behind Achilles in his chariot. We fought back to back. In the evenings I dressed his wounds.

"Leave them," he'd say. "They won't kill me."

His wounds might not have been killing Achilles, but inside he was dying a thousand deaths. It was his mother and his own pride that had led the Greeks into such dire straits. Every night we watched the funeral pyres burning. He could not speak. He just gripped my hand. How I was ever going to let him go, I had no idea.

Odysseus needed less help on the field, for the simple reason that he was less often on it. Most of his work was done in the smoky hull of some ship, trying to come up with a winning plan. No one was more cunning, more able to see opportunities or anticipate obstacles than my friend. The problem was, he couldn't predict how the "O"s might act.

Olympus rang with the clashes between Zeus and Hera, one backing the Trojans and the other the Greeks. Every day in the throne room, Hera petitioned Dad to withdraw his support from the Trojans. Dad hurled abuse at her with the same fury he used to hurl thunderbolts. Hera set her proud chin, pushed out her chest, and stood defiant before the greatest power there is.

I'd never thought much of Mrs. O, but now I stood with her, slipping my hand into hers, making Dad roar louder, but also making him abandon his dais and slam out of the room more quickly. Sometimes semi-circles from Mrs. O's nails were left pressed into the skin of my knuckles, she held me that tightly.

Now and then, to avoid the fighting at Troy and on Olympus, I would visit Athens. It wasn't much of an escape. Throughout the night, bonfires urned along the high walls of the Acropolis. en looked out to sea, balancing scrawny their boney hips, wondering what had happened to all their men. The flickering light cast deep shadows around eyes already dark with worry.

Then, finally, it looked as if the balance might tip. Achilles killed Troy's great hero, Hector, in single combat. The eldest son of King Priam—as selfless as his youngest brother Paris was self-centered—Hector had been the strength of the city. He had not only led the Trojans on the battlefield, his bravery had given courage to young and old behind the walls. His personal conduct, unlike Agamemnon's greed or Achilles' pride, had reassured the Trojans that they deserved victory.

Like fire through dry grass, hope spread through the Greek camp on the news of Hector's death. Just as rapidly, despair withered Troy. With Hector gone and Achilles triumphant, how could the Trojans hold out? Surely, after ten years, the end of the war was in sight.

Relief washed through me. I was sad for Hector, who was a great man, but Achilles, Diomedes, and Odysseus had made it through. If the Trojans now sued for peace and gave up Helen, my boys would go home. Troy, one of my cities, would be humbled—but it would still stand.

It was not to be. A single arrow, fired by none other than Paris from atop his high walls, whistled down and struck my beloved Achilles. The iron tip pierced his right heel. There was nothing I could do and we both knew it. I knelt in the dust where he had fallen and took his hand one last time in mine. Through the distortion of my tears, I watched his fingers loosen their grip. I tried to press them back close again, I tried to make him hold on—but he was gone.

Soon Achilles, like Hector, was nothing but ashes on a pyre.

That night I stood alone on the beach by the Greek camp. Great carcasses of ships bared their ribs to the moon. Their timbers had not been stripped by dogs or vultures, but to build funeral pyres for the men who would never sail them home. I felt like lying down on the sand next to these ghostly monuments just to put my heart down, just to stop having to carry it.

I could lie down and close my eyes, and refuse to ever open them again.

But of course I could not.

I entered a huddle of ships that still had their skins intact. A few men were speaking in low tones. Around them, others were sleeping next to piles of dirty armor. One of the whisperers raised his eyes to me and stiffened.

"Go get some rest now," he said to his companions who had not seen me.

"Odysseus," I whispered.

He pressed his lips together. It would have been a smile in happier times.

"Odysseus," I repeated. "This war has to end."

I didn't say, *because Achilles is dead, and I can't lose you and Diomedes as well. Because what is the use of being the goddess of war strategy if you can't even protect your friends?*

"How?" he asked. "We have lost Achilles."

"And they have lost Hector."

"But they have their walls," he objected.

I smiled. It was a real smile, if one without any joy. Trust Odysseus to stumble on the answer, even when he didn't know it himself.

"I have an idea," I said.

That Horse

Odysseus knew just the man for the job: Epeius. He was a thin, nervous, cowardly man, full of tics and twitches, but he was a craftsman.

"It-it can't be done," Epeius stammered from his seat on the other side of the table, deep within Odysseus' ship. He squinted at the first lines of my drawing in the quavering lamplight, not quite daring to look at me yet not daring to look away. His head wobbled uncertainly on his reedy neck.

Odysseus, seated beside him, snorted, amused.

Diomedes pursed his lips. He was leaning against the wall by the doorway, his head slightly bowed to fit under the ceiling, the only other person in the room.

"Are you telling me I don't know how to do it?" I asked Epeius.

Epeius' eyes flew open in alarm. He shook his head furiously. "N-no, my goddess. N-not at all."

"Fine then, I will show you how." I bent toward him to fill in more detail with a piece of charcoal. He flinched and held his breath.

"Epeius! You're going to have to learn to relax!" Odysseus burst out laughing.

Diomedes scowled at him. "If some Trojan spy hears laughter coming from this ship..."

Odysseus quieted down, but his eyes sparkled. It was so good to see my friend like this again, revitalized with hope.

"Diomedes," I said, "Epeius and I have work to do. In the meantime, you and Odysseus have to steal my sacred statue, the Palladium, from the Trojan citadel. Bring it back here. I will not have it said that a totem of mine failed to protect its city."

Diomedes bowed. He pulled Odysseus out with him. The two of them picked their way unseen to the base of the Trojan walls. This might not have been possible just a short while ago, but it was not only the Greeks who were running out of men.

When they reached the part of the wall directly below the city's citadel where the Palladium was kept, Diomedes crouched down. Odysseus climbed onto his shoulders. He laid his palms against the smooth lower skirt of the wall to help him balance. Then Diomedes straightened up, thrusting Odysseus skyward. Straining up on his toes, Odysseus' fingers found the first foothold in the higher, rougher part of the wall. He pulled himself up, stepping on his friend's head and then on Diomedes' upraised hands for leverage. With a final kick and flurry, he was up and over.

Before long, Diomedes heard the high hiccup of a little owl calling. He looked up and saw Odysseus' head appear over the wall, a darker black against the night sky. He reached out his arms, and Odysseus dropped a heavy parcel into them, wrapped in the folds of a rather smelly cloak. My boys and the Palladium headed back to me.

Safe in the ship, Odysseus re-enacted his

adventure, which seemed to include the slaying of many, many sentries.

Diomedes shook his head. "That didn't really happen," he said.

"How do you know?" Odysseus snapped.

"You didn't have enough time," Diomedes answered, testing the point of his spear with a thumb. "I know how long it takes to kill a man."

"Well," I interrupted, heading off a silly argument. "What's important is that the Palladium is here and not in Troy, so Troy can fall without shame to me. And fall it will, if we follow my plan."

Epeius nodded, as if he'd always been convinced.

It took a few days for Epeius to build my invention and for Odysseus to teach the other Greeks their parts in my plan. Then finally one evening, as the sun sank toward the sea, great ropes were fastened to the remaining intact ships, and the men began pulling them down the beach to meet the rising tide. From behind their high walls, still unnerved by the loss of the Palladium, the Trojans strained to see what was going on. As night fell and the waterline rose, fires sprang up along the beach. The Greeks were putting out to sea, abandoning and torching their camp!

The Trojans stayed behind their walls until morning, watching the fires burn low. The rising sun lit a deserted beach. Apart from the skeletons of a few ships, only one thing remained on the sands—an enormous wooden horse. Carved on its side were the words: *For their safe return home, an offering to Athena from the Greeks.*

"What do you make of this?" King Priam asked Paris. He wished it were his eldest son, Hector, beside him. But Hector was dead. The thought stabbed through Priam like a knife.

"The Greeks are not to be trusted, father. I say we should burn it where it stands."

The Greeks are not to be trusted, thought Priam. *And how trustworthy were you, my Trojan son, stealing your host's wife? I should have shut my doors on you when you returned with your stolen bride. Instead I opened my arms and loved her as my own daughter.*

And now, after ten years, Hector dead. So many dead. The sand on this beach is made from the dust of their bones.

Out loud the king said, "Bring the offering to the citadel. We will dedicate it to Athena in her temple, as is proper."

I felt a pang of regret at these words. Priam was a good man, guilty only of spoiling his youngest son. But there was nothing I could do now. One way or the other, this war had to end.

The Trojans rolled the wooden horse into the city, behind the high Trojan walls that had kept the Greeks out for a decade and—who knows—might have kept them out for all time.

In the belly of the horse rocked and swayed the handful that was left of the Greeks' best men, led by Odysseus. Diomedes was there, his great bulk contorted uncomfortably in the small space. Epeius sat quaking by a trap door that was one of my special touches. It was invisible from the outside and only Epeius knew how to open it. The men remained in their cramped quarters all day, listening to the relieved laughter of the Trojans, tortured by the smell of roasting meat and spilled wine, silent under Odysseus' warning glare.

When night fell, at Odysseus' command, they dropped one by one through the trap door. They made an immediate lunge for the few Trojan sentries still at their posts. Shouts and shrieks filled the air as the Trojans realized what was happening. The clash of metal rang out as the Greeks fought their way to the city gates. Diomedes put his shoulder to the bolt, which was usually drawn by six men. On the other side, the rest of the Greeks were waiting. They had sailed away only far enough to disappear from sight and then sailed back again. With a screeching of metal, the gates opened. The Greeks poured in.

Above the clangs and screams soon came the

roar of fire. Horses whinnied, white-eyed. The high walls of the city danced with the lunging shadows of people being slaughtered. Embers crackled in the air and drifted down to extinguish themselves in pools of blood.

The next morning, the Greeks really did put out to sea. I stood on the deck of Odysseus' ship, with Odysseus and Diomedes on either side of me, and listened to the slap and grunt of men dipping and pulling oars in unison. The salt smell of their sweat rose above that of the ocean. I watched wreathes of smoke drifting toward us across the sands. The air was flecked with grey ashes. Of my once-proud city, nothing remained but blackened ruins. Before long, no man would remember the shape of its stones.

Where You'll Still Find Me

After a while, peace returned even to Olympus. Sure, Dad and Mrs. O still raise their voices now and then, but there seems to be a new bond between them. Once I dropped a knife at dinner, and when I stooped beneath the table to pick it up, I saw they were sitting with his foot on hers. Playing footsie when you've been together for millennia. Just think about it.

The relationship between me and Mrs. O has softened too. We'd both fought on the same side. We'd held hands and stood before the wrath of Zeus. This seems to have earned me the occasional smile from Mrs. O when I pull out my chair and sit down to dinner.

Even things with U.P. are better. U.P. stayed out of the war in the beginning, but he eventually took the Greek side. Like me, he tried to end the war himself. He failed, and later I succeeded. Surprisingly, he didn't hold this against me. Maybe we were all too sick of war to worry who brought the peace. Now U.P. does odd things like pat me on the shoulder and mutter, "You're all grown up." I'm never sure what to make of such behavior, but it pleases Dad enormously.

Dad might be the hardest to understand of all. He is so proud of me. He's forever boring dinner guests with the story of the Trojan Horse, or telling plaintiffs and petitioners that I can end their disputes as surely as I ended the Trojan War. He seems to have completely forgotten that he was rooting for the side I beat.

In any case, we have all learned our lesson. The Olympians will never again go to war against each other. How I wish I could say the same thing about humans, but the Athenians continued to go into battle, and I continued to go with them, protecting each new generation of my boys. They called me Athena Promachos, she who walks—and fights—in front, a name I earned at Troy.

Even greater fame came to me indirectly from Troy. The night that fire consumed the city, a Trojan family stole away. Generations later, they founded another city, Rome. High on a hill they erected a temple to their three most important gods: Dad, whom they named Jupiter; Mrs. O, whom they named Juno; and me, under the name of Minerva.

At first I thought it strange that they would worship the two goddesses who had backed the Greeks against their ancestors. But I guess it does make sense. If we razed your city to the ground, you would want to increase the chances that we were on your side next time.

Under the guise of Minerva, I got to see a lot of the world marching with the Roman armies. Boy could those soldiers march! My fame spread wherever the Romans went, and even to some places they didn't.

You can find statues and emblems of me everywhere. As the symbol of wisdom, I am part of the logos of colleges and universities across the world—in Belgium, Germany, Bulgaria, South Africa, Brazil, England, Scotland, Australia, and the Netherlands. In the United States, I'm even on the great seal of the State of California, sitting on a rock, my shield resting against my knees, looking down at ships anchored off the Californian coast, a miniature bear from the Californian flag at my feet.

But when I'm not on Olympus, you'll most often find me with the Athenians, on the Acropolis that they built for me. When the chatter of the day's tourists has receded and older voices whisper among the stones, I walk here, looking down at the twinkling lights that now spread all the way to the sea. Laughter rises up from the homes and tavernas below me. Olive trees spread their branches in tiny gardens. A warm breeze blows in from the harbor, bending the tufts of sunburnt grass that still push their way through the paving stones, as they have pushed their way for millennia. My temples rise around me, although they are now nostalgic ruins. And I am serene with the ease of belonging in two worlds—both among my family, and among these people who have loved me for nearly three thousand years.

Who Were the Ancient Greeks?

Ancient Greece, more properly referred to as the Ancient Greek World, consisted of independent city states and kingdoms, sometimes allied in leagues, and sometimes at war with each other. What unified the Ancient Greek World was not nationality but culture. Its people shared a language (with local dialects), ate and dressed more or less the same way (with local variations), and worshipped the same gods (plus various local deities).

Many modern countries are land surrounded by sea. The Ancient Greek World was a sea surrounded by lands. As you can see from this beautiful old French map, that sea was the Aegean Sea in the Eastern Mediterranean, and the lands included parts of what are now Italy and Turkey, as well as modern Greece.

To further complicate the picture, in English translations of *The Illiad,* Homer's great and gory tale of the Trojan War, the men who mostly came from west of the Aegean sea to fight the Trojans are referred to as "the Greeks." (We have followed this custom.)

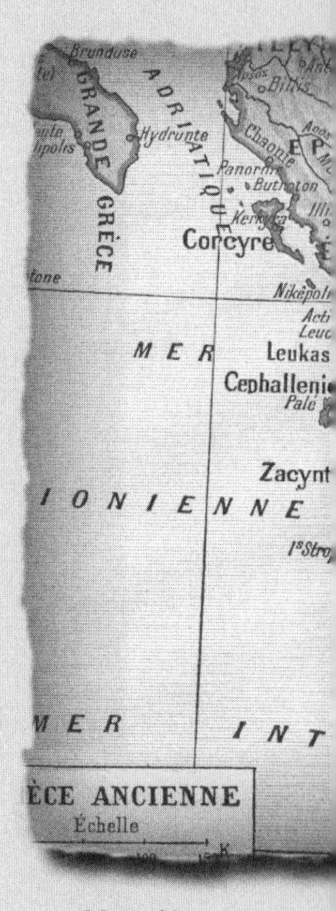

1. Mount Olympus
2. Athens
3. Sparta

Just remember that Troy was also part of the Ancient Greek World. Before Paris betrayed Menelaus by stealing his wife, he was welcomed in Sparta not as a barbarian foreigner, but as a fellow Greek prince.

4. Lydia
5. The Aegean Sea
6. Troy

Athena's Extended Family

The Ancient Greeks lived in a world colorfully populated by immortal beings. There were not only the gods, but also other divine races such as the Cyclopes and the Titans; less powerful spirits of the woods and waters (nymphs), the deep oceans (nereids), artistic endeavor and knowledge (the muses), revelry and exuberance (the satyrs); and darker beings who brought vengeance (the furies).

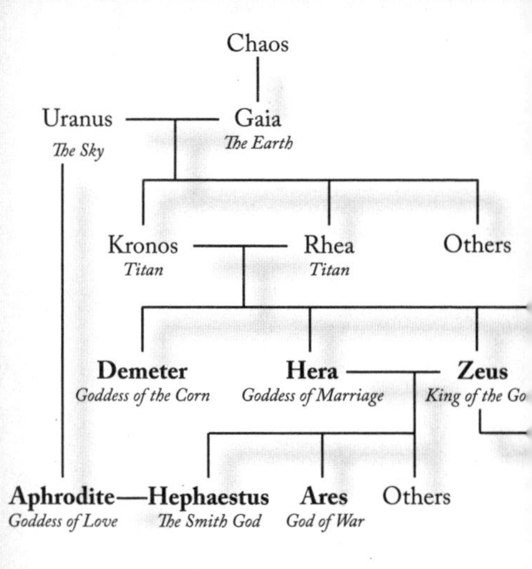

Of all the immortals, the most powerful were the Olympians. But it may surprise you to know that the Olympians were not the first gods. Rather, they were the third and fourth generation.

The first goddess, Gaia, arose out of Chaos. She had a son, Uranus, whom she married. (Marrying your family was not considered odd or repulsive behavior for gods and goddesses.)

A simplified family tree of the Greek gods, showing the relationship between the Twelve Olympians (names shown in bold).

Gaia and Uranus had many children, of three different races. They were the *Cyclopes,* three giants, each with a single eye; the *Hekatonchires*, three monsters, each with a hundred hands; and the twelve *Titans*, six male and six female.

Uranus was appalled by his children and tried to lock them away in Tartarus, a remote region of the Underworld. This upset Gaia. She urged Kronos, the youngest Titan, to rebel. He did, cutting off Uranus' genitals and casting them into the sea. There they turned into a white foam, from which rose Aphrodite, Goddess of Love and Beauty.

Aphrodite—or Venus, as she was known to the Romans—rising from the waves. A famous painting by the Renaissance master Sandro Botticelli.

Kronos, now the supreme god, locked his brothers the Cyclopes and Hekatonchires back into Tartarus. He then married his sister Rhea. Together, they had six children. However, Kronos was afraid that his children would overthrow him, just as he'd overthrown his own father, so he swallowed each child as it was born. Determined to save her children, Rhea gave Kronos a stone to swallow instead of her last baby, Zeus.

Rhea gives Kronos a rock. Drawing from a bas-relief on an early Roman tomb.

Hidden from his father, Zeus grew up. When he was strong enough, he returned in disguise and became Kronos' cup bearer. With Rhea's help, he gave Kronos a drink that made Kronos throw up the stone he'd swallowed all those years ago, followed by all of Zeus' elder brothers and sisters.

This began an inter-generational war that came to be known as the Clash of the Titans. Zeus and his siblings released the Cyclopes and Hekatonchires, and with their help, won the war.

To divide the dominion of the universe between them, Zeus and his brothers drew straws. Hades became King of the Underworld; Poseidon, Lord of the Seas; Zeus, Lord of the Skies and King of the Gods. As the new supreme ruler, Zeus set up his court on the cloud-covered peak of Mount Olympus.

Mount Olympus, Greece.

The Twelve Olympians

The Ancient Greeks agreed that the most important and powerful gods and goddesses resided on Mount Olympus. They also agreed that they were twelve in number. What was not resolved was *which* twelve gods they were.

It might seem odd that the membership of The Twelve was left so vaguely defined, but the Ancient Greeks were comfortable with a constant reinterpretation and elaboration of their mythology. Their playwrights added detail and altered plot lines. Local deities were sometimes absorbed into the worship of the national gods, adding different facets to their personalities.

Some of the Olympians shown on the pediment of the National Academy in Athens.

1

2

3

4

The gods and goddesses who were *always* counted among The Twelve were: Zeus, Hera, Poseidon, Aphrodite, Ares, Artemis, Apollo, Hephaestus, Demeter, and Athena. Hestia, Hermes, Hades, and Dionysus were sometimes counted and sometimes not. Several configurations were accepted. The one we have used is a common one.

1. ***Apollo:*** *He can be identified by the lyre he holds.*

2. ***Artemis:*** *Although she is not shown with her bow, the intimacy between the twins is visible.*

3. ***Athena:*** *She is unmistakable with her helmet, spear, and shield. She stands to the right of her father.*

4. ***Zeus:*** *The King of the Gods is depicted on his throne.*

5. ***Hera:*** *She wears a royal diadem and her head is modestly covered, as befitting a married woman.*

6. ***Aphrodite:*** *She is shown with her son, Eros, and deep in conversation with Ares.*

7. ***Ares:*** *Like Athena, the God of War wears a helmet.*

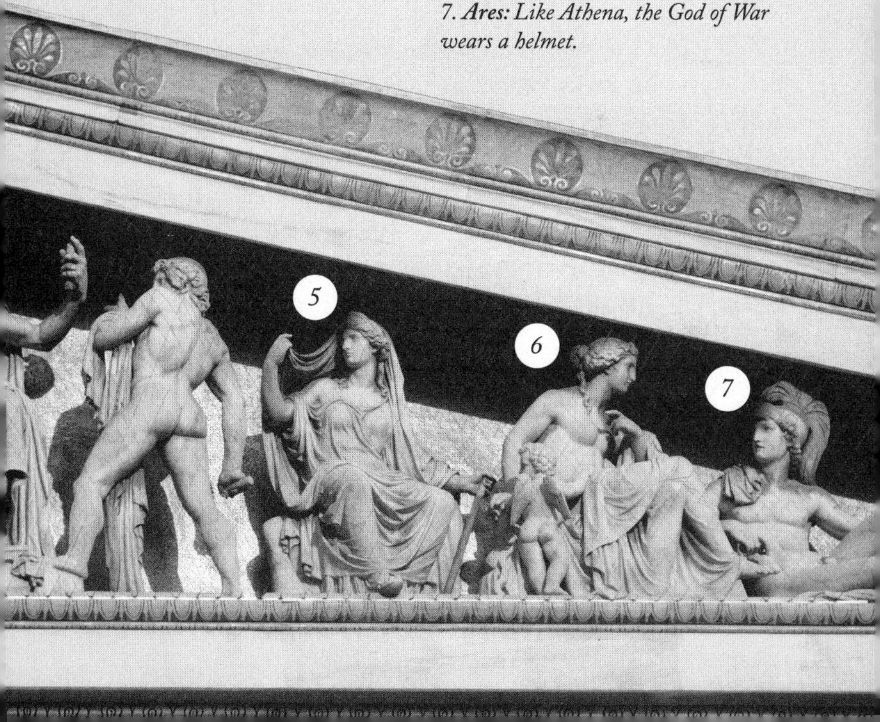

5

6

7

What Athena Wore

Athena is usually shown in the armor of a *hoplite*, a Greek infantryman. She wears a helmet with a horsehair plume. On one arm she carries the large round shield, or *hoplon,* from which the hoplites got their name. She is armed not with a sword, but with a spear, the primary weapon of Greek *phalanxes*—disciplined military units that fought with their shields overlapping, pushing and thrusting with their long spears. Protecting her chest is either a *cuirass*, a bronze breast plate, or her *aegis*—a magical goatskin garment tasseled with snakes or with gold, and bearing the Gorgon Medusa's head, a gift from Perseus. Sometimes the Gorgon's head is depicted in the middle of her cuirass instead, or in the center of her shield.

All this armor is worn over a long robe, either a *peplos* or a *chiton*. An earlier garment, the peplos was made of wool. It was folded over at the top so a flap hung down around the top of the body. The chiton gradually came to replace the peplos as standard Greek dress for women. It was a lighter garment, made of linen, and worn without the fold, so it draped closer to the body and was more revealing. Athena is shown robed in either, but every year at the *Panathenaea*, the main festival in her honor given in Athens, she was given a new peplos by her adoring people.

Men wore shorter tunics than women did. Cut above the knee and draped over only one shoulder, they were called *exomis*, meaning "off the shoulder." Both men and women wore *himatia*, long cloaks draped over the left shoulder.

This American statue of Athena, which adorns the Athenaeum Press building erected in 1895 in Cambridge, Massachusettes, shows the goddess in a peplos and himation, with her helmet, spear, and aegis.

An older statue of Athena, showing her carrying her shield.

Remains of a statue depicting a man in an exomis.

What Athena Ate

The Greek gods were thought to exist on *ambrosia* and *nectar*, and foods that were sacrificed to them. It was never very clear what ambrosia and nectar were, or even whether they were solid food or a drink. In Homer's epic, *The Iliad*, ambrosia was the food and nectar the drink of the gods. We've followed this convention.

As for the rest of Athena's diet, the Ancient Greeks kept a calendar of festivals that involved regular sacrifices to the gods. The most common form of sacrifice to the Olympians was the

A bas-relief sculpture from the southern frieze of the Parthenon showing a bull being led to the sacrificial altar during the Panathenaea, the thanks-giving celebration to Athena.

thigh bones of an animal, wrapped in fat. The animal would be killed on a high altar, and then the bones and fat burnt. The smoke would rise to the heavens as food for the gods. Light-colored animals were especially prized. In contrast, funerary sacrifices to Hades favored dark animals, slaughtered on the ground and burned entirely.

In addition to meat, there were sacrifices of corn, cakes, and fruit. *Libations*, ritual pourings and sacrifices of wine, were routinely made in the morning and evening, before every meal, or any time wine was drunk. During dinner parties called *symposia,* which usually featured three great jugs of wine, the libation before the first jug was made to the Olympians.

A painting on a "red figure" bowl showing a boar being lifted onto an outdoor altar for sacrifice. As well as being fed during festivals, the gods claimed a portion of every hunt, catch, and harvest.

What Everybody Else Ate

As you may have guessed from the story about Athena winning Athens with the gift of the olive tree, olives and olive oil were very important to the Ancient Greek diet. The Ancient Greek lands, as a whole, were very poor agriculturally. The soil around Athens in particular was too thin to grow cereals. The olive became Athens' main agricultural product. Wheat and barley, used to make bread, had to be imported.

For most ordinary people, bread and olives, supplemented with cheese, eggs, and vegetables, would have been the usual fare. Meat was a luxury. Many people would have been able to enjoy meats only during festivals such as the Panathenaea, which usually involved animal sacrifices. The meat not offered to the gods would then be distributed among the people.

Although some cattle were grazed on the sparse hillsides of Ancient Greece, goats were much more common, being famously able to glean a living from the most rugged and inhospitable terrain. Goats supplied the Ancient Greeks not only with some meat, but also with cheese. Butter and milk were reserved for use in medicines.

For those who lived on the coast, a wide variety of fish and shellfish was available. Some of this bounty was also sold inland, either preserved by pickling, drying, or salting, or transported "live." (With no refrigeration or ice, food poisoning must have been all too common.)

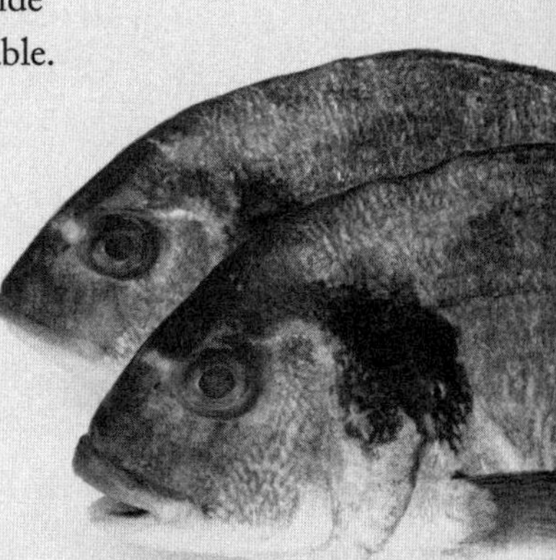

As for drink, the Ancient Greeks were said to have invented wine. Certainly it was a major industry, with trade routes criss-crossing the Ancient Greek World. The Ancient Greeks always drank their wine watered down. Drinking wine "straight" was considered barbaric, and such behavior was thought to lead to madness.

Wine was an important part of Ancient Greek culture, and was part of daily religious rituals.

Athena's High City

One of the most exciting aspects of Athena's mythology is that her high city, or *acropolis*, still exists. If you are lucky enough to be able to visit Athens in Greece, you will be able to visit her temples and hear ancient voices whispering among the stones.

The crowning glory of the Acropolis, and indeed of Ancient Greek art and architecture, is the Parthenon. Built at the height of Athenian power, from 447 to 432 BCE, the Parthenon replaced an older temple to Athena—one of several that crowded the hill top. It held a statue of Athena called the *Athena Parthenos*, designed by the famous sculptor and architect Phidias. Unlike the simple and sacred wooden statue that was bathed and dressed during the Panathenaea festival every year, the Athena Parthenos appears to have had more of a practical function than a religious one: it was dressed in 44 *talents* (1,100 kilograms or 2,400 pounds) of pure gold. The gold was made to be removable. Athena was literally a bank her people could draw from in times of need.

The Acropolis rises above modern Athens, dominated by the Parthenon. If you look closely, to the left you'll see people climbing the Propylaea, *the great flight of steps leading up to the "high city."*

One other famous statue of Athena is known to have graced the Acropolis—the *Athena Promachos*, or "Athena who fights in front." It was a colossal bronze statue, thirty feet high, that showed Athena battle-ready, with her spear raised. It was erected in 456 BCE, to thank the goddess for her help in the Battle of Marathon.

Leo von Klenze's depiction of what the Acropolis looked like at its peak, with the Propylaea leading up to the Athena Promachos, and the Parthenon looming.

Athena Now

Athena in her Ancient Greek form, and as the Roman goddess Minerva, is one of the hardiest survivors from classical mythology. Her image graced the coins of Ancient Athens. Her statue rose above the Capitoline Hill of Rome. Across the Western world, as far east as Romania, her statues still stand. On the western edge of the world, in the United States, she speaks to Benjamin Franklin in the eye of the US Capitol Building's rotunda, and appears on the Great Seal of California with the California bear tamely at her feet. Nor does our fascination with Athena show any sign of waning. A full-size replica of the Parthenon and the statue of Athena Parthenos was recently built in Nashville's Centennial Park.

Athena in the US Capitol Rotunda.

Athena in front of the Austrian Parliament Building.

The Great Seal of California.

The reconstruction of the Athena Parthenos in Nashville, Tennessee.

Myth, Fact, or Fiction?

This is a novel based on ancient myths. Myths were never meant to be a fixed accounting. They were always open to reinterpretation and retelling. You might be interested to see how much of this telling was based on a skeleton of established myth, how much of it was made up or fictionalized, and how much of it was informed by research and facts.

My Father's Headache

Established Myth	Fact	Fiction
Athena was born from Zeus' forehead, fully grown and clad in armor.		
		Zeus' headache and the events of the day leading to Athena's birth.
To release Athena, Hephaestus split open Zeus' head with an axe.		

You Can't Choose Your Family

Established Myth	Fact	Fiction
Hephaestus created dwellings for all the gods and goddesses on Olympus.		
		The interaction between Athena and Hephaestus.
	Greek women wore long robes called *chitons* or *peplos*. Athena is usually shown wearing one under her armor.	
The Twelve Olympians dined together regularly as a family on Mount Olympus.		
		Conversation and events during dinner.
	The Ancient Greeks made offerings of burnt meat, fat, and bone to feed the gods on Olympus.	

A City in My Name

Established Myth	Fact	Fiction
Hephaestus spent much of his time on Lemnos and Demeter spent a lot of her time on Earth.		
		Athena felt lonely and Zeus gave her a job.
	The Ancient Greeks saw their gods mainly as a form of insurance.	
		Poseidon petitioned Zeus for the patronage of Athens.
Athena beat Poseidon in a contest for Athens by giving the city an olive tree, while Poseidon gave the city a salt spring (or in some myths, the first horse).		
		The events on the day of the competition.
	Details about the location and architecture of the Athenian Acropolis.	

The Vote

Established Myth	Fact	Fiction
		The Olympians gave Athena the cold shoulder after the contest for Athens.
Athena invented the plough, the rake, the ox-yoke, the horse bridle, and the chariot among other things.		
	The Ancient Greeks, and especially the Athenians, were famous for beautiful "black figure" and "red figure" pottery.	
The gods voted that Poseidon had given the better gift, while the goddesses voted for Athena.		
		The dinner on Olympus.
		Zeus' conversation with Athena and his warning to avoid getting too close to mortals.

Too Close

Established Myth	Fact	Fiction
	"Ancient Greece" included states like Lydia in modern Turkey.	
	In Ancient Greece, girls and women spent most of their lives weaving in the *gynaikon*.	
		Athena's interactions with the Lydian women and Arachne.
Aphrodite had a magic girdle that made her irresistable.		
To escape Apollo, Daphne prayed to be turned into a laurel tree.		
Athena turned Arachne into a spider for claiming to be the better weaver.		
		The confrontation between Athena and Arachne, and the rationale behind Athena's actions.

A Lesson

Established Myth	Fact	Fiction
		Athena withdrew from mortals and gods, and became depressed.
		The friendship between Hephaestus and Athena.
Hephaestus fathered Erichthonius when Athena visited his workshop.		
Erichthonius was variously described as human, part-human-part-serpent, or a serpent.		
Athena adopted and raised Erichthonius.		
	The Athenians believed a sacred snake lived in Athena's temple.	
		Hephaestus suspected the gossip was meant to teach Athena a lesson.

My Boys

Established Myth	Fact	Fiction
		Athena moved from Olympus to Athens.
	The Athenians fed Athena's sacred snake and saw omens in its behavior.	
Athena was the friend and protector of Greek heroes.		
Athena helped Perseus to find Medusa, and Jason in his quest for the Golden Fleece.		
		Jason spent his last night alive with Athena.
Thetis dipped Achilles in the River Styx to make him immortal, but she left a mortal area where she was holding him.		
		The relationship between Athena and Achilles, and their conversation on the bank of the river.

A Feathered Friend

Established Myth	Fact	Fiction
		Athena's life in Athens and her love for her city.
		Athena missed her family.
		The appearance of Athena's owl.
	There are small owls called *Athene noctua* that live in the cliff walls of the Acropolis.	
Athena was associated with owls, thought the wisest of birds. She is often depicted with one, and owls became one of her symbols.		
		Athena's return to Olympus and her reception from the other Olympians.

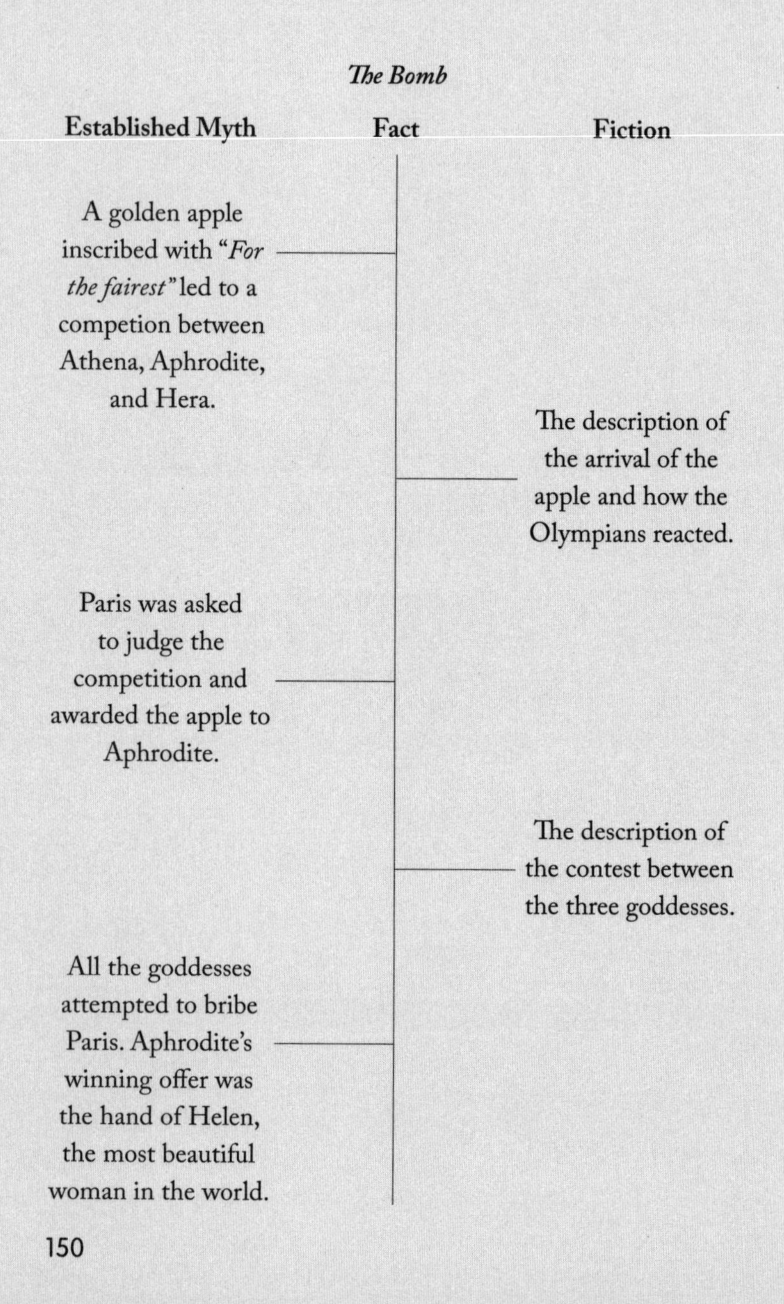

The Bomb
Established Myth
Fact
Fiction
A golden apple inscribed with "For the fairest" led to a competion between Athena, Aphrodite, and Hera.
The description of the arrival of the apple and how the Olympians reacted.
Paris was asked to judge the competition and awarded the apple to Aphrodite.
The description of the contest between the three goddesses.
All the goddesses attempted to bribe Paris. Aphrodite's winning offer was the hand of Helen, the most beautiful woman in the world.

Fine Print

Established Myth	Fact	Fiction
		Athena woke to find Olympus in uproar.
		The conversation between the Olympians and events at breakfast.
Paris visited Sparta for nine days and ran away with Helen when Menelaus was called away to a funeral.		
Helen took five serving women, most of the palace treasure, and gold from Apollo's temple.		
Hera warned Menelaus and sent a storm to toss Paris' ships.		
		The description of the Greeks preparing for war.

War

Established Myth	Fact	Fiction
The Trojan War was fought for ten years.		
Apollo got involved when Agamemnon refused to return his priest's daughter.		
		The description of the priest's interaction with the Greeks.
		The description of Apollo's reaction on Olympus.
Hera and Athena banded together to help the Greeks.		
Athena intervened when Achilles thought of killing Agamemnon.		
		Athena's relationship with Achilles. Her reaction to events.
Achilles sulked in his ships. His mother made matters worse by asking Zeus to support the Trojans.		

Established Myth	Fact	Fiction
		The description of Thetis' visit to Olympus.
		Scenes of Athena helping her friends.
Athena stood with Hera in support of the Greeks against Zeus' wrath.		
		Athena's conflicted emotions about Troy and her motive for supporting the Greeks.
		Athena's visit to Athens.
Achilles returned to the fray and killed Hector, Troy's hero.		
Achilles was in turn killed by Paris' arrow.		
		Athena mourned Achilles.
		Athena visited Odysseus in his ship.
Athena gave Odysseus the idea of the Trojan Horse.		

That Horse

Established Myth	Fact	Fiction
Epeius was chosen by Odysseus to build the Trojan Horse.		
		The friends met in Odysseus' ship.
Athena's statue, the Palladium, was stolen from Troy, removing the goddess' protection.		
		Odysseus and Diomedes' adventure.
The Greeks pretended to abandon camp.		
		King Priam's thoughts and regrets over the war.
The Greeks used the Trojan Horse to enter Troy, then sacked and burned the city.		
		Athena surveyed the ruins of Troy the next morning from Odysseus' ship as the Greeks departed.
	For many years, no one would remember that Troy ever existed.	

END

Glossary

Acropolis	Citadel built on high ground; "upper city"
Aegis	Protective magical garment or shield
Chiton	Linen tunic that falls to the ankles
Cuirass	Armor covering the torso; also called a breastplate
Divan	Couch-like furniture for sitting
Exomis	Short tunic worn by men
Gynaikon	Women's room or quarters
Himatia	Rectangular cloak worn over the left shoulder
Hoplite	Citizen infantry of Ancient Greek city-states
Hoplon	Round shield
Libation	Ritual pouring of a liquid as an offering to a god
Nereid	Sea nymph
Nymph	Minor female nature deity
Omniscience	The capacity to know everything
Phalanx	Military formation used in Ancient Greek warfare
Peplos	Long woolen garment worn by women
Polis	Greek word for "city"
Propylaea	Monumental entrance to the Acropolis in Athens
Panathenaea	The most important of all the festivals at Athens; it was held to honor Athena
Satyr	Minor diety usually depicted as half man, half goat; companions of Dionysus
Symposium	A dinner party
Talent	An ancient unit of mass

Bibliography

Adkins, Lesley and Adkins, Roy. *Handbook to Life in Ancient Greece.* Facts on File, Inc. 1997.

Allan, Tony and Matiland, Sara. *Titans and Olympians: Greek & Roman Myth.* Time-Life Books, 1997.

Apollodorus. *The Library of Greek Mythology.* Translated by Robin Hard. Oxford University Press, 1997.

Buxton, R.G.A. *The Complete World of Greek Mythology.* Thames & Hudson, 2006.

Finley, M.I. *The World of Odysseus.* The Folio Society Ltd., 2002.

Garland, Robert. *Daily Life of the Ancient Greeks.* (The Greenwood Press "Daily Life Through History" Series). Greenwood Press, 1998.

Graves, Robert. *The Greek Myths.* The Folio Society Ltd., 2000.

Homer. *The Illiad.* Translated by Robert Fagles. Penguin Classics, 1990.

The Oxford History of the Classical World. Boardman, John; Griffen, Jasper; Murray, Oswyn; Editors. Oxford University Press, 1986.

World Mythology. Willis, Roy; General Editor. Henry Holt and Company, Inc., 1993.